TO

BE

TAUGHT

IF

FORTUNATE

BECKY

CHAMBERS

HODDER &
STOUGHTON

First published in Great Britain in 2019 by Hodder & Stoughton
An Hachette UK company

I

A CIP catalogue record for this title is available from the British Library

Hardback ISBN 9781473697164

Typeset in Sabon by Palimpsest Book Production Ltd, Falkirk, Stirlingshire

Printed and bound in Great Britain by Clays Ltd, Elcograf S.p.A.

Hodder & Stoughton policy is to use papers that are natural,
renewable and recyclable products and made from wood grown in sustainable
forests. The logging and manufacturing processes are expected to conform
to the environmental regulations of the country of origin.

Hodder & Stoughton Ltd
Carmelite House
50 Victoria Embankment
London EC4Y 0DZ

www.hodder.co.uk

To Emily, who doesn't have to read this, but did make me think the right thing.

Please Read This

If you read nothing else we've sent home, please at least read this. I ask knowing full well that this request is antithetical to what I believe in my heart of hearts. Our mission reports contain our science, and the science is by far the most important thing here. My crew and I are a secondary concern. Tertiary, even.

But all the same, we do have a lot riding on someone picking this up.

You don't have to rush. This file will have taken fourteen years to reach Earth, and assuming that we have the good luck of someone reading it right away and replying straight after, it'd take *that* file another fourteen years. So, while we can't wait around forever, the urgency – like so many things in space travel – is relative.

You could, I suppose, skip right to the end. You wouldn't be the first person to do such a thing, and honestly, that's where the bit that affects us most will be laid out. And maybe, if you already know who we are and what we're about – if you're someone who sent us here, perhaps – you can do that and still understand. But even if that's the case, I do think the *why* of what we need from you is important. I'm biased, of course, and doubly so: Not only is this account about me and my crew, but we're scientists. We live and breathe *why*.

It's been fifty years since we left Earth, and I don't know whose eyes or ears this message has reached. I know how much a world can change within the bookends of a lifetime. Causes shift and memories blur. I also don't know how much *you* personally know of the universe beyond our home planet. Perhaps you're one of the knowledgeable sorts I've already mentioned, who can rattle off spaceflight history better than even I can and who shares the same goals as me. Or perhaps you're someone who lives outside my bubble. Perhaps this is all new to you. When I use words like 'exoplanet' or 'red dwarf', do you know what I mean? This is not a test, and I absolutely do not judge if terms such as these mean nothing to you. On the contrary, I want to speak to you as much as I want to speak to my peers – maybe even more so. If I ask what I'm asking only of people who agree with me at the outset, with whom I already share a dream and a language, then there's no point in asking at all.

For this reason, I'll do my best to speak to expert and novice both. I likewise feel it important to start from the beginning, so that the context of our situation is clear. I doubt what I write will be objective. I will almost certainly contradict myself.

I do promise that I'll tell the truth.

My name is Ariadne O'Neill, and I'm the flight engineer aboard the OCA spacecraft *Merian*. My crewmates are mission specialists Elena Quesada-Cruz, Jack Vo, and Chikondi Daka. We're part of the Lawki program, a broad ecological survey of exoplanets – that is, planets that do not orbit our sun – known or suspected to harbour life. Our mission (Lawki 6) is focused on the four habitable worlds in orbit around the red dwarf star Zhenyi (BA-921): the icy moon Aecor, and the terrestrial planets Mirabilis, Opera, and Votum. I'm currently stationed on the surface of the last on that list.

I was born in Cascadia on July 13, 2081. On that day, it had been fifty-five years, eight months, and nine days since a human being had been in space. I was the two-hundred-and-fourth person to go back, and part of the sixth extrasolar crew. I'm writing to you in the hope that we will not be the last.

4

Aecor
(and Earth)

I never knew an Earth that was unaware of life elsewhere. The Cetus probe scooped up bacteria-laden samples from Europa's geysers twenty-nine years before my birth; the first rover photographs of fossil arthropods on Mars arrived while my parents were still in trade school. I don't know what it was like in those lonely years before, when our view of Earth's place in the universe was one of a solitary haven, an oasis in a galactic desert. In some ways, I wish I did. I wish I could've been there the day the first positive results were radioed back from Cetus. I wish I could tell you what it was like to be in one of the old mission controls or research labs or newsrooms, learning in real time with the rest of the planet that our small worldview had been magnificently blown apart. But by the start of my life, just three decades later, extraterrestrial life was common knowledge, something every kid took for granted. Humans are nothing if not adaptable.

Another wish: that I could tell you I always wanted to be an astronaut. That'd be a much better story, wouldn't it? Some of my colleagues could (and can) claim that. An entire life set in motion by the sight of Saturn's rings through a sidewalk telescope, or a furious sense of purpose imbued the instant they saw those first fuzzy images of a cloud-flecked blue-green exoplanet. I can claim none of those inspirations as my own. I was four when the Tarter space telescope photos came back, and I do actually remember being shown them. My mother lifted me onto her lap in front of her tablet. Her voice was hushed with wonder, and she held me tight.

'Look, honey,' she said. 'That's a planet from around a different star. It's got air and oceans just like we have.'

What I said next is lost to time and the fluff of memory, but what I do recall clearly is utter nonchalance. The picture was boring, and while the factoid that came with it was new and somewhat interesting, I was four. *New and somewhat interesting* applied to about ninety percent of my day, in everything from the development of a scab, to a cartoon I'd never seen, to an unexpected flavour of juice at lunch. It's difficult to assign value to discovery when you haven't sorted out the parameters of reality yet. As such, the significance of the first photographic confirmation of a habitable exoplanet was lost on me. I suppose every childhood is one of blind assumptions.

My parents had an apartment on the twelfth floor of a complex overlooking the Fraser river. That sounds nicer than it was. Urban crush was all I knew, and the closest access I had to nature were the hydroponic planters on our boxy balcony, where my father grew the vegetables we ate for dinner. A hydroponic planter is a far cry from the real outdoors, but it's an ecosystem all the same. I would sit out there for hours in the hot city air, fascinated by the insects that had been likewise drawn to green and growing things. They were a small miracle, those bugs – tiny, wondrous monsters, completely incongruous with the concrete blocks that surrounded us, miniature beasts that appeared like magic and belonged in places far wilder than my father's bell pepper crop. There were beetles and bees, spiders and caterpillars. I watched them flit and rappel from leaf to leaf. I let them crawl on my palm. I marvelled at how something so small had found its way to a location that seemed impossibly high up even for me, the unfathomable giant sharing their space. They had their own dramas, their own goals. They did not *need* me, like a dog or a goldfish might. It was that independence, that complete separation from the human realm, that I loved about them most.

Some insects are born twice, in a sense. First, an egg is laid. Eggs are the given path for most species on Earth, and among larger animals who reproduce this way, this is a simple affair. The egg hatches, an infant emerges – a duck, let's say – and its form is not terribly different than that of its parents. A baby duck is still recognisably a duck. It will get bigger and more hormonal and lose its endearing fluff, but it swims and waddles and pecks. For insects, the process is more complicated. Let's take the moth as an example. A larva emerges from the egg; we know this as a caterpillar. This creature has legs, organs, a mouth – everything a living critter needs. It's perfectly adapted for its current business, which is eating everything in sight and trying to stay hidden from predators. It walks and eats and walks and eats and walks and eats, until one day, it stops. It finds a branch or a leaf. It wraps itself in a protective net of protein. And then, improbably: it dissolves. The caterpillar disintegrates into organic goo, leaving only a few scant essentials intact. In a matter of weeks, the goo recombines, creating another form entirely. Once the creature's body is remade, a second hatching occurs, one that reveals a creature so different from its previous state that if you hadn't witnessed the stage of metamorphosis, you'd make the entirely reasonable assumption that caterpillar and moth were two different species.

Habitable exoplanets may have been lost on me then, but metamorphosis never was. It has always been a thing of beauty to me, the fluidity of form.

Waking from torpor is not my favourite experience. On the scale of discomforts, I'd put it on par with a moderate hangover, or the kind of cold where your sinuses creak if you press on your face. The actual sensation feels like neither of those things. Physically, I feel a little stiff, a little weak, but otherwise fine.

Waking is more of a *mental* discomfort, a period in which your consciousness has to reassert itself after years of dormancy. Keep in mind that medically-induced torpor is not the same as sleep. Sleep conveys the passage of time, even if you don't dream. Not so with torpor. First you're awake, then you're not, then you're back . . . but something's missing. Something's missing, and you'll never be able to put your finger on what.

As soon as the *Merian* established orbit around its first target, a signal was sent from the navigation computer to our crew's torpor chambers. An automated system added a chemical solution to our nutrient drips, and that solution made its way to our respective brains, where it began the business of waking us up. I am told this process takes about an hour, but from my perspective, it happened in an instant. Light. Shapes. Confusion. I had to walk myself through the basics, as if I were reviewing every fact I'd learned during infancy. *I have hands. I have a mouth. Those things I see are colours. I'm Ariadne. I exist.* Then came memories, and context, and finally, a smile.

We're at Aecor.

I began to unpack the proverbial cotton from my mind, and walked myself through protocol. First, I pulled on the tabs that freed my wrists from their soft fabric restraints, then undid the ties around my waist and ankles as well. This may sound macabre, being tied up inside what amounts to a high-tech shipping crate, but the restraints are for a good cause, and removing them by yourself is a breeze. They're snugly attached to the sides of the torpor chamber, keeping me suspended in the middle of the container while I'm unconscious so that I don't float into the sides. This is far preferable to waking up with bruises all over.

Once my limbs were free, I hit the button that opened the chamber door. The light in my room was low, but I winced all the same as my eyes remembered how to adjust themselves. Torpor chambers regularly wash their occupants, but a daily spray of cleaning solution isn't the same as a proper bath. My eyes, nose, and mouth were all crusty around the edges. Twenty-eight years without a real scrub will do that to you.

My hair, shaved before launch, had grown well past my shoulders. My nails had reached a hideous length as well, about what you'd expect after two years of no clipping. That's about how much I aged in twenty-eight years of transit – two years. Torpor slows you down, and interstellar travel at half the speed of light further stalls the clock, but neither presses pause entirely. Cells divide and the heart keeps beating. We buy ourselves time while in torpor, not immortality.

I opened the hygiene kit, which some clever interior engineer had bolted to the wall within arm's reach of my chamber. Nail clippers were the first item I retrieved, followed by a tiny collection bag. I pruned myself, returning my digits to usefulness. Curved keratin shards floated unattractively before me; I hid them away in the little bag as quickly as I could. My unruly hair would have to wait, but I took an elastic band from the kit and tied back my mermaid-like floating locks. The ground teams really do think of everything.

One by one, I removed the electrode patches that covered me from face to feet. Their steady pulses had kept my muscles from atrophying, and for that, I was grateful. Next, I removed the nutrient drip from my arm, bandaged myself, and collected the few drops of blood that had floated free. I then took a breath, readied some therapeutic profanities, and removed the catheter from the place where catheters go.

Ah, the glamour of space travel.

I could hear the faint rustle of my crewmates going through the same checklist of waking. The walls aboard the *Merian* are thin, but there *are* walls, and that point's key. I've seen stills from classic movies in which space-travelling crews are put to sleep, but their chambers or pods or what have you are always lined up side by side, these grim rows of morgue-like containment. Let me be clear on this point: when you've woken up from nearly three decades of induced unconsciousness, and every orifice has gunk around it, and your nails look like talons, and your skin smells like a cross between a freshly-washed hospital bathroom and an abandoned pen at a zoo, and you've just pulled a tube wet with urine out of yourself . . . you need a minute alone. And that's only taking basic hygiene and vanity into consideration. There's an even more important psychological matter at hand during this time.

The mirror.

Once you remember who and what and where you are, your first impulse upon leaving torpor is to *look*. But just as waking up after a visible surgery can be jarring, so, too, can be those first moments taking in your altered body. You're different. You need a moment to prepare, and likely several moments to process, and you definitely don't need to be working through all of that in a group setting. And so, every astronaut's cabin has a full-length mirror, which is yours and yours alone. The mirror is not facing the torpor chamber. It's on the wall to the right of it, out of your line of sight but visible the minute you decide to float forward. The mirror knows you're anxious to see yourself – *but take your time*, it says. *I'm here when you're ready, and not a second before.* It is the kindest object placement I've ever seen.

On the chance that our methods have been forgotten or misrepresented – or you simply never learned about them – let's take a moment to discuss somaforming.

Say what you will about *Homo sapiens*, but you can't argue that we're a versatile species. On Earth, we can survive a decent swath of both heat and cold. We eat a mind-boggling variety of flora and fauna, and can radically change our diets according to need or mood. We can live in deserts, forests, tundras, swamps, plains, mountains, valleys, shorelines, and everything in between. We are generalists, no question.

But take us away from our home planet, and our adaptability vanishes. Extended spaceflight is hell on the human body. No longer challenged by gravity, bones and muscles quickly begin to stop spending resources on maintaining mass. The heart gets lazy in pumping blood. The eyeball changes shape, causing vision problems and headaches. Unpleasant as these ailments are, they pale in comparison to the onslaught of radiation that fills the seeming void. In the early decades of human spaceflight, six months in low-Earth orbit – a mere two hundred miles up – was enough to raise your overall cancer risk a few notches. The farther you head into interplanetary space, away from the gentle atmospheric shores of Earth, the worse the exposure becomes.

Human spaceflight was stalled for decades because of this, crippled by the technological nut that could not be cracked: how do you keep humans alive in space during the length of time it takes to reach other planets? We beat our heads against the drafting table, trying to build tools that could do what our anatomy could not. We wrapped our brains around algorithms, trying to create artificial intelligence that could venture to other worlds for us. But our machines were inadequate, and our software never woke up. We knew there was life on other worlds, yet we couldn't leave our own front yard. And while probes and space telescopes shed ever more light on our galactic neighbourhood, there's only so much you can see looking through a peephole. To properly survey a place, you need boots on the ground. You need human intuition. You need eyes that can tell when something that looks like a rock might be *more* than a rock.

It ended up being far easier, once the science matured, to engineer our bodies instead.

We don't change much – nothing that would make us unrecognisable, nothing that would push us beyond the realm of our humanity, nothing that changes how I think or act or perceive. Only a small number of genetic supplementations are actually possible, and none of them are permanent. You see, an adult human body is comprised of trillions of cells, and if you don't constantly maintain the careful changes you've made to them, they either revert back to their original template as they naturally replace themselves, or mutate malignantly. Hence, the enzyme patch: a synthetic skin-like delivery system that gives our bodies that little bit extra we need to survive on different worlds. If I were to stop wearing patches, my body would eventually flush the supplementations out, and I'd be the same as I was before I became an astronaut (plus the years and the memories).

Somaforming is an elegant solution, but not an immediate process. If enzyme patches are still used medically, you know this already – if you're diabetic, for example, and can't produce insulin on your own. But if you've never worn a patch (or if they're old news by now), you might imagine something more dramatic than is accurate. I once spoke to a kid at an outreach event who was very disappointed to learn that applying a patch does not result in instant transformation (complete with an animation sequence and a theme song, I'd imagine). We astronauts are not superheroes, nor shape-shifters. We're as human as you. While our bodies are wondrously malleable things, they still need time to adjust. Life-saving organ transplants or helpful medicines can often be met with some level of physiological resistance; the same is true of somaforming. It is more preferable, by far, to be unconscious while your body sorts itself out.

Again, I'm as biased as can be, but I believe somaforming is the most ethical option when it comes to setting foot off Earth. I'm an observer, not a conqueror. I have no interest in changing other worlds to suit me. I choose the lighter touch: changing myself to suit them.

At first glance upon waking at Aecor, I did not look particularly different. The enzyme patch on my shoulder – regularly swapped out during torpor by a helpful robotic mechanism – had been supplying me with the same sort of basic astronaut survival kit that I'd maintained since my first training mission in low-Earth orbit. My blood produces its own antifreeze to survive the extreme temperatures of both space and ground. My skin passively absorbs radiation and converts it into sustenance. These additions I have had for a long time. But as my weightless body shifted in microgravity, drifting like kelp in a gentle sea, a new supplementation made itself clear.

Glitter.

I can think of at least one lab tech back home who would frown at me for calling it glitter. Technically, what I possessed was synthetic reflectin, a protein naturally found in the skin of certain species of squid. But . . . come on. It's glitter. My skin *glittered*, and for a moment, I felt childlike glee, like I'd emptied a bunch of craft supplies on myself, like I'd had my face painted at a carnival, like I'd flown here in a cloud of pixie dust. But it was practical, the astroglitter. Aecor is roughly as far from its star as Uranus is from our own, which makes for a sun no bigger than a fingerprint in the sky. Night and day do not look dramatically different. Here, glitter served the same purpose for us that it does for sea-dwelling animals back home: it catches and refracts light. While we would be clothed for the majority of the work day, being able to spot your crewmates' glittery faces on a pitch-black ice field certainly wouldn't hurt. We also needed to limit the use of work lights on said pitch-black ice fields, because light means heat, and we didn't want to cause melt. And indoors, reflectin means less energy spent on indoor lighting, which is great when on a world where solar panels are useless and everything runs on battery.

Besides which: *I glittered*. It felt like a damn shame to put my clothes on, but I managed it all the same.

Chikondi was the first person I saw that day, and his face was far more startling to me than my own. To my memory, I'd said goodbye to him about an hour prior, but there he was, scruffy-faced and sparkly-skinned . . . and noticeably older. He is the youngest of us, and that two years of ageing had a more marked effect on a face in its twenties. He was thinner, too, and so was I, but I'd spent so much time mentally preparing for how *I'd* be different that I hadn't thought much about how my friends might change.

Clearly, Chikondi felt the same, because he stared at me for a moment before ending the awkwardness with a laugh. 'Good morning,' he said.

'Good morning,' I returned. 'Sleep well?'

'I had this weird dream. I was helping my brother reorganise a massive library, and the books were written in gibberish, and suddenly I realised they weren't books at all but *cake*—'

I frowned. Nothing about his conscious mind should have been active. I began to mentally rifle through what this could mean, everything that could've gone wrong with the chamber, the malfunctions I'd obviously missed during inspection, the unforeseen consequences this could mean for his brain . . .

Chikondi smiled slyly at me. 'Ariadne, I'm kidding.' He laughed again.

I cuffed his shoulder gently, then flipped my head down, floated past the ladder, and pushed myself along the walls with my hands. 'So you *are* all right, right?'

'Fantastic,' Chikondi said. There was a pause. 'I hate catheters.'

I nodded in solidarity. 'Truer words.'

We found Elena in the control room, starting a systems check. I wondered if she'd needed much time to look at herself, or if this was all old hat by now. Elena's the oldest of our crew by a minimum of nine years, and thus, her résumé has more to boast. She was part of the Eridania 8 mission to Mars, as well as the first to set foot on Ceres. This was not her first rodeo. But whatever her feelings about her body were, her keenness to get to work could not have been more plain. I'd seen that same glint in her eyes every morning we'd done field training together, every time she'd strapped on her boots for a hike or filled a bag with sample jars. I had a feeling that to her, otherworldly skin was just a sign that things were about to get good.

'Good morning,' Chikondi said to her.

'Good . . .' She glanced at a monitor. 'Afternoon, actually.'

'Right,' Chikondi said. Aecor's day was eight of ours, but we were still keeping Earth time.

Some of us were, anyway. Jack came floating downstairs a half hour later, late as always. I've been on crews with Jack since my early days at OCA, and we've long kept close company outside of that, but in that moment, I'm not sure I'd have recognised him in a crowd. I'd never seen him with long hair, or a beard that was anything but artfully groomed.

He looked at us each in turn, and burst out laughing. 'You all look like shit,' he said.

'So do you,' Elena said, matter-of-fact.

'Yeah.' Jack stuck his nose into his shirt and grimaced. 'Ugh.' He touched the thick bun bobbing at the crown of his head. 'This needs to get murdered. Might keep the beard, though. Chikondi? Wanna be beard buds?'

They grinned at each other from within their respective thickets. 'Sure,' Chikondi said. 'But I think yours constitutes a fire hazard.'

Jack chuckled heartily. 'You're not doing much better, mate.'

I floated over to the comms monitor. 'We've got files coming in,' I said.

'Anything urgent?' Elena asked.

Any information OCA had sent us would be fourteen years out of date, but even problems that old were well worth knowing. I skimmed over the download list. No protocol updates, no emergency notices. I shook my head. 'Parameters are unchanged,' I said. 'Mission is a go.' I watched the progress bars inch forward, byte by byte, and the sight sparked a warmth within me, the same sort I'd got whenever a drone had dropped supplies at the OCA mobile base in Antarctica, or when my parents had sent me care packages while I was away at school. When the world you know is out of reach, nothing is more welcome than a measurable reminder that it still exists.

In terms of formal training, I'm not a scientist. I'm an engineer. I build the machines and provide the propulsion that gets scientists where they need to go. I'm a support class, in essence. I've always felt most comfortable in that role. The day I applied for trainee work at OCA – just shy of nineteen – I walked in the door of the Vancouver campus with no thought beyond keeping my feet firmly on the ground. I imagined a life of craning my neck back as my work vanished into the clouds. I had no idea how far I would go – but then, I'm not sure OCA knew that about itself, either.

It's understandable why humans stopped living in space in the 2020s. How can you think of the stars when the seas are spilling over? How can you spare thought for alien ecosystems when your cities are too hot to inhabit? How can you trade fuel and metal and ideas when the lines on every map are in flux? How can anyone be expected to care about the questions of worlds above when the questions of the world you're stuck on – those most vital criteria of home and health and safety – remain unanswered?

Keeping probes and satellites spinning is one thing; keeping astronauts alive is quite another. In the throes of the Great Shift, there were none with sufficient stable resources – human, monetary, or material – to keep that latter work going. Even if there had been, those who held the purse strings so often had motives beyond the glorious dawns they claimed to support. If you wanted the funding and facilities for spaceflight, you could either appeal to your government, whose support for the sciences might prove hollow as soon as there wasn't a war to win, or to a corporate entity, which would chase scientific progress provided that there was a positive correlation to their bottom line.

So much for the benefit of all mankind.

For the people who worked on those programs – the astronauts, yes, and the breakthrough scientists, yes, but also the thousands upon thousands of everyday engineers, mathematicians, doctors, lab grunts, and data hounds whose names and stories are lost to us – these were not the futures they were chasing. They'd been sold on a vision of discovery and progress accessible to everyone. A global mindset. An enlightened humanity. Instead, they found that dream inextricably, cripplingly anchored to the very founts of nationalistic myopia and materialistic greed that said dream was antithetical to. I imagine many despaired at this reality, and perhaps lost heart.

But our history remembers those that did the opposite. People of science, after all, are stubborn beyond the point of sense.

Have you ever been in a place where history becomes tangible? Where you stand motionless, feeling time and importance press around you, press *into* you? That was how I felt the first time I stood in the astronaut garden at OCA PNW. Is it still there? Do you know it? Every OCA campus had – has, please let it be *has* – one: a circular enclave, walled by smooth white stone that towered up and up until it abruptly cut off, definitive as the end of an atmosphere, making room for the sky above. Stretching up from the ground, standing in neat rows and with an equally neat carpet of microclover in between, were trees, one for every person who'd taken a trip off Earth on an OCA rocket. It didn't matter where you from, where you trained, where your spacecraft launched. When someone went up, every OCA campus planted a sapling.

The trees are an awesome sight, but bear in mind: the forest above is not the garden's entry point. You enter from underground.

I remember walking through a short tunnel and into a low-lit domed chamber that possessed nothing but a spiral staircase leading upward. The walls were made of thick glass, and behind it was the dense network you find below every forest. Roots interlocking like fingers, with gossamer fungus sprawled symbiotically between, allowing for the peaceful exchange of carbon and nutrients. Worms traversed roads of their own making. Pockets of water and pebbles decorated the scene. This is what a forest is, after all. Don't believe the lie of individual trees, each a monument to its own self-made success. A forest is an interdependent community. Resources are shared, and life in isolation is a death sentence.

As I stood contemplating the roots, a hidden timer triggered, and the lights faded out. My breath went with it. The glass was etched with some kind of luminescent colourant, invisible when the lights were on, but glowing boldly in the dark. I moved closer, and I saw names – thousands upon thousands of names, printed as small as possible. I understood what I was seeing without being told.

The idea behind Open Cluster Astronautics was simple: citizen-funded spaceflight. Exploration for exploration's sake. Apolitical, international, non-profit. Donations accepted from anyone, with no kickbacks or concessions or promises of anything beyond a fervent attempt to bring astronauts back from extinction. It began in a post thread kicked off in 2052, a literal moonshot by a collective of frustrated friends from all corners – former thinkers for big names gone bankrupt, starry-eyed academics who wanted to do more than teach the past, government bureau members whose governments no longer existed. If you want to do good science with clean money and clean hands, they argued, if you want to keep the fire burning even as flags and logos came down, if you understand that space exploration is best when it's done in the name of the people, then the people are the ones who have to make it happen.

And we did.

Their names are on the root-level glass, those original twelve, in font no bigger than any other. So are the names of everyone who has ever given anything to the cause. Doesn't matter if you're a millionaire who kept our lights on every year or somebody who donated a spare tip to the cause a grand total of once. The amount a person can spare is relative; the value of generosity is not. All those little cobbles were enough to pave the road back to Luna, then to Mars and the asteroid belt and beyond.

I tried to find my name on the wall – I'd given all my beer money to an OCA employee I'd heard speak at school four months prior – but the lights came back before I located myself. I was returned to the world of tendrils and worms, fungus and rock, locked together in an unbreakable web. Viewed in this way, you can never again see a tree as a single entity, despite its visual dominance. It towers. It's impressive. But in the end, it's a fragile endeavour that can only stand thanks to the contributions of many. We celebrate the tree that stretches to the sky, but it is the ground we should ultimately thank.

A hundred and fifty odd years of people making spacecraft that can land themselves on other planets has made my responsibilities as pilot more of a backup plan than anything else. I absolutely need to be there with my hands on the proverbial wheel in case something goes wrong, and I approach that job with deadly seriousness. Even if nothing ever *does* go wrong, I have to prepare as though it might.

On Aecor, it did not. We descended into the atmosphere without a hitch. The air allowed us through, and physics led the way from there. My body travelled through a spectrum of gravity – first nothing, then a fast crescendo of sluggish weight that transitioned into ever-increasing lightness. The change plateaued in an unfamiliar state, one that was lighter than Earth, but heavier than its moon. This was a gentle world, one that wouldn't drag you down or trip you up. It was a small delight, that point-six-G. The gravitational equivalent of a sip of cold soda or a quick shoulder rub.

The *Merian*'s landing legs had barely finished deployment before Jack was undoing his safety restraints. 'Dibs on shower,' he said.

The rest of us groaned in protest. Showering is an utterly impossible activity in a weightless environment, unless you like the idea of floating in the middle of a spray of spherical blobs that go everywhere but where you want them to. We hadn't been able to properly clean ourselves up since coming out of torpor, and we were all aching for a turn in the stall.

'You don't want a haircut before you shower?' Elena asked, unbuckling her own restraints. Hair we *could've* addressed in microgravity, but then you have to use a vacuum cleaner. It's so much easier when the clippings fall straight down.

Jack pointed at Elena in agreement. 'Dibs on clippers.'

'Okay,' she said, heading down the ladder. 'But first haircut means last out the hatch.'

'Oh, that's not fair,' he said, following after.

I punched buttons. 'All systems nominal, if anyone cares,' I said. I wasn't actually fussed in the slightest. If anything, I took it as sign of their trust in the *Merian*, which, by extension, was something of a compliment to my ability to keep an eye on her.

Chikondi flashed me a thumbs up as he descended the ladder. 'I care.'

'Thanks, Chikondi.' I finished my landing sequence, and followed the others down the ladder. It's always odd, being able to only move downward in a space I floated in minutes before.

Despite our collective grunge, there was a fizzy impatience in the air as we buzzed our heads and took turns in the compact shower. There was a whole *moon* waiting outside, but first, we had to *bathe*. If you want to see highly-trained astronauts devolve into twitchy five-year-olds, this is the time to witness it. Nobody wants to take a bath before they go out to play.

We gathered in the cargo hold after we'd finished putting ourselves together. Jack produced a six-sided die from his pocket and set it on a storage crate. 'Who's feeling lucky?'

Elena picked up the die and turned it between her fingers. 'High or low?'

'Low?' Jack asked, looking around for our agreement. We all nodded. 'Low. One is best.'

Elena rolled, and scoffed. Five.

Chikondi went next. Three.

Jack followed him. He laughed as the die came to rest. Another three. 'Beard buds,' he said to Chikondi, and gave him a high five.

'You didn't keep your beards,' I said.

'Thank God,' Elena added.

'Doesn't matter,' Jack said. 'Beard buds are more of . . .'

'A state of mind,' Chikondi said.

'A state of mind,' Jack affirmed.

I rolled my eyes, then the die.

I stared.

Two.

I kept staring, even as Jack hooted and Chikondi clapped me on the back.

I'd be the first out the door.

If the OCA media archives are still around, you can find footage of Lawki 6's launch party. The campus hall was decked to the nines, the tall ceiling under which I'd attended so many meetings almost unrecognisable behind its costume of banners and coloured lights. The place was packed, as was to be expected. In addition to the project teams and the project teams' families, you'll see the press, and the *press'* families, and citizen supporters from all over the world.

If you watch the footage, you'll see us, too: four people weaving our way through a sea of humanity, shaking hands and giving hugs and accepting gifts. You'll see Elena, in her sharp suit and her cresting hair, the consummate professional, as effortlessly approachable in a throng of a thousand as if she'd been in a lecture hall of one hundred, or at a family dinner of ten. You'll see Jack, a rakish grin on his face and his jacket rumpled just so, getting high on the OCA Oceania crowd going batshit for their Melbourne-raised hero. You'll see Chikondi, handsome as a portrait and the most nervous I think he's ever been in his life. He loves people, and I wouldn't categorise him as shy, but he's infinitely more comfortable in an audience than in the spotlight. That's why you'll see me at his side – the one in the blue dress, whispering stupid jokes in his ear to keep him smiling in a sea of cameras. I'm smiling, too – partly because his laughter fuelled my own, partly because this was not my first time at a PR circus, mainly because I *was* having a good time. A party is a party, and when it's a party for you and the people you love best, it's hard not to enjoy yourself.

If you watch closely, though, you might catch a moment when my face falls. I don't know when in the evening it happened, but it's the thing I remember most. That's the moment when I saw my family in the crowd: my parents, my brother, my sister-in-law, my little nieces. I knew they'd been there, but I hadn't expected to see them in the context of my public rounds on the floor. They cheered for me, my family. They cheered and called my name and jumped up and down. But I could see the pain in their eyes, too, a pain that matched the same I'd buried behind my practised smile.

A return to Earth is a key component of all the Lawki missions. OCA was vehemently opposed to putting people aboard a one-way flight. Our mission is to catalogue, not to colonise. Returning to the world you'd laboured to gather knowledge for is psychologically vital. You had to remember who you were doing the work for. You had to know the finite spacecraft that carried you would not be your final home. Without a restful full-circle ending awaiting you, an astronaut under duress might decide to cut the cord, to make a home on a world that was not theirs. Lawki 6 would return to Earth, our mission briefing unequivocally declared.

We'd just be doing so in eighty years.

We astronauts are taught to compartmentalise the realities of interstellar flight. The launch party is a public celebration; the family day that begins the following morning is a time of private grief. There is no schedule that day; our PR shepherd was not tapping his foot and checking his clock while holding a pack of tissues. The day belongs to you and yours.

I will not detail here what I did or said on family day, or repeat the words that still echo in my ears. That belongs to me alone. I'm not going to perform that part of myself for anyone. I won't say, either, how it went for my crewmates (though we've unpacked that baggage among ourselves many, many times). I'll explain family day for you in the most astronautical way I know how: a simple briefing.

You get in a car and you go to a place of your choosing. A park, maybe. A beach. A house rented for the occasion, complete with doors that lock and blinds that lower.

You hold everyone, as tightly as you can.

You tell them you love them.

You tell them you know.

You tell them goodbye.

You cry. A lot.

You keep crying after you're back at campus. You cry until you run to the sink and vomit. You cry through that as well.

You wonder if you're a bad daughter, a bad friend, a selfish asshole placing her own intellectual wankery above the living, breathing people who poured everything they could possibly give into her, and were rewarded with the sight of her walking away forever.

You never answer that question, and you never will.
You strap into your rocket ship anyway.
Somehow, you leave.

My heart pounded as I put on my suit. We wear suits, of course:
TEVA suits for the ground – that's Terrestrial Extra-Vehicular
Activity – and the infinitely bulkier EVA suits – plain old Extra-
Vehicular Activity – for spacewalks. TEVA suits are partially for
our own protection, but mostly to protect the world from
ourselves. This is another misconception people have about
somaforming – the notion that our supplementations mean we
can stroll around alien environments in brilliant nudity, passing
through any biome with no more impact than a soft breeze. It's
a romantic image, but one that would be reckless in the extreme.
Even after washing, human skin is laden with bacteria that are,
to us, good and necessary, but would wreak havoc in a new
ecosystem. We exhale bacteria, too, in the micro-droplets of
moisture that travel through our airways. Symbiotic microbes
aside, there's no telling what human contaminants could do to
an environment. Is our skin oil toxic to the life there? Do we
shed allergens? Are we passively poisonous? There's no way of
knowing. Plus, *we* could get sick, too, and that'd be the end of
the mission (and likely ourselves). Hence, suits.

This was not my first step off Earth. I'd spent a summative
year and a half at the New Millennium Lunar Base. I felt
transcendent the moment my first spacecraft touched down
there, and had an echoing thrill every morning I woke up in my
bunk and remembered *oh my God, I'm on the Moon*. But in
some ways, the experience was not so removed from travelling
on Earth. The Moon was not a mystery, but a place visited
by many others before me. It's difficult for me to explain this
feeling, because I'm afraid of coming off as *yep, went to the
Moon, no big deal*. The Moon is incredible, I assure you. I felt
my daily share of reverence. But I felt a similar reverence, a

related reverence, when I stood at the rim of the Grand Canyon for the first time, or stood breathless and shivering atop Mount Fuji. Places I had learned of and longed for, suddenly manifest around me. I felt the same on the Moon, in what I thought was the end-all-be-all. I thought I had reached the summit of wonder, that all natural spectacles would enchant me in much the same way.

Not so.

I descended the ramp. My thoughts were dizzy, dreamlike. I was so overwhelmed that I was afraid I wouldn't remember the moment later. But I did. I do. I'll never forget it.

Impossible quiet waited beyond the airlock, as if this moon were holding its breath with me. My boots clunked lightly on the ramp, each foot headed a little further down. The sound changed – not the clap of machine-made metal, but the soft crunch of ice. I could feel it give ever so slightly beneath my weight, then hold fast. Endless ice surrounded me, untouched and undisturbed. A flawless canvas. A smooth block of clay. And it *looked* more like clay or mud than the water I knew it to be comprised of. Thanks to the red-light spectrum bestowed by the sun above, the ice did not appear white or blue, but rather shiny black. It reminded me more of a lava field than anything.

I stood there, without thought or words. Despite the inviting bounce of low gravity, I remained stock-still. On Luna, I visited the Apollo sites, as all astronauts do. It's our pilgrimage, our rite. I viewed Neil Armstrong's footsteps, preserved behind their protective glass domes, and as I stood in that same lunar dust, I felt the way I had on Earth when I visited the Cave of Altamira and raised my palm so that it nearly touched the painted print left by someone thirty-six-thousand years prior: a tiny link in a mighty chain.

Aecor was different. My footprints would not stay there, I knew. I was standing on ice, not rock, and the same geysers that had polished the frozen ocean smooth would do so again, given time. But I was forging a *new* chain, and the immensity of that is a feeling I doubt can be matched.

Jack broke my reverie. 'One small step, hey, Ari?' he said, reading my mind. I turned and looked. All three of my crew were waiting in the airlock, and I suppose I'd been standing there for a while, because they were laughing at me. Well, not Elena. She let out a bit of a chuckle, but it came with a knowing smile. She'd been the first to stand on an asteroid, after all. She understood.

Like any good guests, we carefully checked our surroundings before setting up our temporary home. A probe can scout out a good spot for you to plant your spacecraft, but it's only when you're on the ground that you can tell if you're about to unroll a habitat module into a puddle, or worse yet, onto something's home. I sent everybody away from the lander, each in a different direction, walking counter-clockwise. We scrutinised the ground below us for anything better left alone. We do our best to leave no trace.

It's difficult to know where to draw a line with that. If you overthink it – a classic human trait if ever there was one – you start to fall down a rabbit hole of potential disasters. What if the lander itself crushed something? What if the noise of landing scared something away and disrupted their breeding season? What if the exact place where your craft landed is where two bacteria of separate species met for the first time, and what if their meeting would have resulted in a symbiosis that would have led to the emergence of a new species, and you, you bastard, just wiped out that entire reality?

I used to stay awake at night stuck in these worries. But if you live by that logic, you can never take another step. The way I look at it, if the impact of one house-sized object is enough to disrupt an entire evolutionary thread, that thread didn't have much of a shot to begin with. A spacecraft landing is no different than a boulder shifting, a meteor crashing, a tree falling. And unlike those objects, we do leave, and we do clean up after ourselves. We try to be mindful tenants and ethical observers, to have as minimal an impact as possible. *As possible.* At some point, you have to accept the fact that any movement creates waves, and the only other option is to lie still and learn nothing.

These moral quandaries nagged at me from afar as I examined the ground. I initially turned on my headlamps, but this made for a jarring juxtaposition. Unlike the weak sunlight straining from above, my lamps emit a full white-light spectrum, thus creating colours around me that hadn't existed earlier (think like shining a blacklight in a dark room). Under my mobile pools of light, the black ice became white, stained with streaks of yellow and brown. It was disorientating, in that moment, so I found it easier to let my eyes adjust to Aecor in its native state.

'Anybody else find any vents?' Chikondi said over the comms. 'I've got a little one here. Man, I wish I could smell it.'

Jack was less than enthused. 'I'll take you to a storm drain when we get back home,' he said. 'Throw some old eggs in it. It'll be about the same.'

That's the thing about these majestic icy moons. The surface ice is a lovely postcard, but the liquid water beneath stinks to high heaven. It's an entire ocean of undisturbed brine, warm as a bathtub, brimming with bacteria, chock-full of the remnants of every birth and death that has ever occurred within it. It is, as evidenced by Chikondi bemoaning his clean canned oxygen, a smell only a biologist could love.

'Are vents something we need to worry about?' I asked. I found one of my own, a small, steaming hollow leading to depths unknown.

'No,' Elena said. 'We want vents, within reason and at a safe distance. Think of them like a pressure valve.'

'Yeah,' Jack added. 'Something without holes might pop.'

'And no one wants that,' Chikondi said.

'No one wants that.'

Visual check complete, we brought out the auger to check the ice's thickness, to make sure that it would hold our craft for an extended period. Green lights all around. At last, it was time for the fun part.

Inflatable habitat modules are one of my favourite inventions. The *Merian* comes equipped with two of them – one for the greenhouse, one for the clean lab – each attaching to an airlock on the side of the capsule. They nearly double our living space, but pack away into containment units about half the size of a small car. All we have to do is remove the storage covers, roll out the nigh-indestructible fabric, hit a button, and watch them go.

Even with the modules extended, the space within our habitat is roughly that of a spacious single-family home. You might think that spending years in such a dwelling might start to feel claustrophobic, but consider the fact that ours is the only human home – the only building at all – on any world we travel to. Even the most rural humans can't understand what it means to be standing on an entire planet that has no cities, no streets, no artificial structures at all. If you've been lucky enough to go to a wildlife preserve or some other wide-open space, you might have a glimmer of what that means. The absence of machine sounds. The awesome, fragile humility of knowing you're the only human around for miles. But even in such places, even up remote mountains or on the longest backpacking trips, you know that somewhere out there, there's a road. There's a ranger station. There's a hotel with a bathtub and a breakfast buffet.

Not so on Aecor. Not anywhere off Earth. As of yet, we have found no other life forms that build cities or machines. When standing on one of these quieter worlds, you know that the entire sphere, in every direction, is wilderness. Go too far from your lander, and your surroundings quickly remind you that you're only an animal, and that there's a reason our forbears invented tools and walls.

Faced with such enormity, I find the close quarters of the *Merian* to be a massive comfort. When you spend day after day after day doing fieldwork in an environment of endless expanse, the most welcome sight in the world is a snug bunk behind a locked door.

I enlisted my crewmates in monitoring the module inflation with me. We took up posts, watching every crease and corner for hidden tears.

'I love these so much,' Jack said, watching with satisfaction as the marshmallowy cylinders puffed themselves up. I, too, enjoyed the sight, but I was even more eager for what came next: unpacking our toys.

Have you ever been camping? If so, when you bought your first batch of gear, did you have a moment where you laid it all out in front of you and marvelled at the smorgasbord of clever little bits? The tiny tinderbox? The quick-drying towel? The pop-out kitchenware? The pocket-sized tool that contained a magnifying glass and three knives and a fish scaler you'd never use? That is how I feel every single time we set up our surface labs. Storage space is at a premium in any spacecraft, and being able to fully kit out multi-purpose research facilities obviously requires a lot of stuff. But this need is handily met aboard the *Merian*, which boasts a cargo hold crammed with a treasure trove of scientific necessities. Microscopes, thermometers, altimeters, light sensors, camera traps, pH probes, turbidity tubes, handheld sonar, ovens, quadrats, shovels, sample dishes, 3D printers, tweezers, molecular scanners, core samplers, seismic monitors, wildlife blinds, tape measures, audio recorders, aerodrones, hydrodrones, gloves, masks, tags, slides, and more goggles than you can shake a stick at, all as lightweight and compact as the best minds on Earth could make them, all securely stowed away in perfect crates with perfect labels in perfect rows.

It is immensely satisfying.

Modules deployed, we went back inside and unpacked our bounty, forming an industrious bucket brigade. 'Greenhouse first?' Chikondi asked.

'Lab first,' Elena said.

'Aw,' he replied. The clean lab was the bigger task, but he was eager to begin the business of growing vegetables. You might think this was a pragmatic desire – radiation alone doesn't give us all the nutrients we need to survive, and the sooner we start seedlings, the sooner we get snacks. But no, Chikondi just wanted to start playing with plants, just as I knew Elena was itching to collect steam from the vents, just as Jack wanted to go on a hike to search for rocks. Me, I was already in my happy place. Landing had worked, the suits worked, the modules worked, the perfect crates were being unpacked. In order to do science, you need tools, shelter, and a means to get where you're going. I was responsible for all of these. I was building a trellis where good work would grow. There was nothing I wanted more than that, nothing that brought me more pride.

'Do you miss coffee?'

I asked this of Jack as he awoke beside me. We'd moved his cot into my cabin the night before, as we do sometimes. Or vice versa. Or not at all.

Jack considered as he blinked at the painted metal ceiling. 'Nah,' he said, scratching his stubble. His answer wasn't surprising in the slightest. Jack doesn't miss having to eat throughout the day. Back on Earth, he was always the sort of walking disaster who would eat heartily – prodigiously – when you put food in front of him, but would otherwise neglect it entirely, getting lost in work or play until the onset of a roaring headache and a foul mood reminded him to shove a protein bar into his face so he could keep going. Of all of us, he had the easiest time letting go of the contentment of a full belly. For Jack, adopting an alternative means of sustenance was liberation. He couldn't wait to be free of the need to stop for lunch.

I got up and got dressed. Jack stretched like a cat, folding his arms behind his head, savouring his simple pillow as if he were in a fine hotel.

'It's so still,' I said, peeking out the porthole. Ice stretched unendingly around us, barren and beautiful. 'Good day for anybody who wants to find some rocks.'

There's nothing in existence Jack loves with more ardent passion than rocks, except for dirt, especially dirt that has *become* rock, and *especially* if that rock has fossils within. He nodded approvingly at my comment, but made no motion to end his dozing.

There was a period in our life together when I would've pestered him to get up, asked him if he knew what time it was. Those days have long passed. I know how a morning goes for Jack. He'll lie there until the last possible second, saunter into the lab with all the urgency of arriving at Sunday brunch, then do work so good that it doesn't matter what time of day it happens in. Jack is a swagger, a wink, a final aced even though he's never been to class, a joint smoked in bed after a day in the field, a rock climbed and an ocean swum. He knows he's good at his job and just flat-out good-looking, and he uses both to get away with murder. The only thing more infuriating than that is how much of a sucker I am for it.

I looked at myself in the mirror and rubbed my scalp. The shave I'd given myself wasn't particularly even. I picked up my tablet from the cabinet nearby, and glanced over the day's schedule. 'You know we've got to file check-ups today, right?' I asked. The torpor system keeps tabs on our health, but you can't really tell if your internal systems are chugging along as they should be until they're getting some normal use. After we make camp and get settled, full physicals are the next order of business.

Jack gave me a thumbs up from where he lay. Whether this meant *yes* or *I do now* was anyone's guess, but ultimately immaterial. Jack would remember. Patch check-ups are something even he wouldn't mess around with.

I left my cabin and climbed down the ladder to the deck below. I found Elena in the control room, reviewing that morning's data on the big screen. I could tell from the flush in her cheeks that she'd already been outside that day, walking at her usual steady clip from weather station to weather station, making sure her instruments were in good order. A green light on a monitor is never enough for her. Elena likes visual checks. She likes tangibility. The wind and sky were ephemeral enough, she told me once. If she's going to study them, she wants to feel them.

'Anything good?' I asked, my palm cupping her shoulder. I share her cabin sometimes, too. She doesn't move her cot into mine. Elena likes her own space.

I knew her responding expression well – that sure-footed half-smile, oozing satisfaction, a look that says she has her shit together better than anyone ever has or will. 'Numbers are *always* good,' she said. She looked at me, her gaze shifting to the sides of my head. 'Your hair could use some help.'

I laughed. 'Yeah, I was hoping you could—'

She was already out of her chair, waving me toward the bathroom. When Elena tells you to follow her somewhere, you go. Doesn't matter if it's down a dark cliff or into an unfamiliar alley or just across the hall. When Elena decides where she's going, all you can do is try to keep up.

We fell into our usual positions: me on the floor, her on a stool with clippers in hand and legs making a chair around me. She put a towel around my shoulders and guided my head downward, pushing gently against the crown of my skull with her palm. The clippers buzzed against my scalp. Little tufts of shorn hair tumbled onto our respective legs. She has strong legs, which used to run marathons and were never too proud to dance if asked. I felt safe there, as I always do, and was profoundly glad of that feeling. Thirteen conscious years of living with and working with and leaning on Elena, and to this day, she still intimidates the hell out of me. In a good way.

'Do you miss coffee?' I asked.

Elena let out a short moan. 'God, yes. Do you know how much more I'd get done around here if we had caffeine?' She nudged my head to the side and worked around my ears. 'I miss hot chocolate, too.'

'Oh, man.' I closed my eyes, remembering warm Christmases with family, cheap packet mixes in school, gratifying thermoses on camping trips. 'With marshmallows.'

'Fuck marshmallows. Cinnamon or go home.'

I laughed, and so did she. She finished my haircut, brushing the tickling scraps off my neck, and looked at herself in the mirror. 'I could use a touch-up too, I think,' she said. I didn't offer to return the favour. Elena cuts her own hair, and had already started to do so over the sink. 'I'll clean up,' she said. 'You know to file check-ups today, right?'

'Yeah.'

'I already did mine, but I don't think Chikondi has yet.'

'Is he up?'

She *mmm*'d assent, running the razor over her head. I left her to it, and headed back to the ladder. I didn't need to guess where my remaining crewmate was.

I climbed down, past life support and on to the cargo hold. I went into Airlock A, through the metal walls of the spacecraft and into one of the inflatable modules. A wave of humid air hit me, and my eyes squinted as they adjusted to the brightness of the grow lights.

Chikondi stood at the greenhouse's workbench, inspecting his first cuttings under a microscope and singing quietly along with his headphones. I walked up beside him and casually watched him work, waiting for the inevitable delight of the moment when he realised I was there.

The moment came, and it was perfect. Chikondi jumped about a foot.

'Ariadne!' He took off his headphones, pushed me in mock anger, and laughed at himself. 'How long have you been there?'

'Just a minute.'

Chikondi shook his head. 'That's a terrible way to say good morning.'

'I'm very sorry,' I said, not sorry at all.

He looked at me, waiting.

'Good morning, Chikondi.'

'*Good morning,*' he returned pointedly. 'Here, look—' He picked up a tiny leaf of fast-growing spinach, engineered to go from seed to salad in days. 'I saved this for you.'

I took the offering and held it up. The stem had split itself, forming two little leaves side by side. 'It's twins.'

'It's a mutant!' he said happily. No further explanation for why he had set it aside was needed. The leaf was a mutant, and mutants were cool, the end. He reached out, broke one of the leaves off, and popped it into his mouth.

I did the same with my half. 'That's a tasty mutant,' I said.

He nodded enthusiastically. 'I think this nutrient mix is a winner. This crop's already coming out much more robust than our training batches. I'll write up the changes I made in our next report. When's it due?'

'Tuesday. Hey, speaking of mutants and protocol—'

He stared at me for a moment, searching. 'Check-ups,' he said. 'Right.' He looked a little despondent at the idea of leaving his workbench, but nodded with a responsible sigh. Chikondi, unlike Jack, *would* forget, especially if something as enticing as plant samples were at hand. 'Let's do it.'

We went back up the ladder together, chatting about the success of his fertiliser. He'd been working on this project for weeks before launch, and I'd stayed up many a night with him in our shared campus home, letting him bounce thoughts about potassium and nitrogen off of me. Chikondi's not interested in sex – with me or anyone else – but when he comes to my cabin to talk, we engage in another kind of sharing, one that's every bit as good and every bit as intimate.

'Me first, or you first?' he asked as we entered the medical bay.

I headed for the supply cabinet. 'You first?'

He hopped up on the exam table, and we followed protocol, step by step. I checked his weight, his vitals. I could feel him relax under my touch, as I'd done with Elena as she cut my hair. It made me feel steady, that reciprocal trust.

'Do you miss coffee?' I asked as I listened to his heartbeat. We have a pulse reader that's more accurate than the stethoscope, but Chikondi's the one who taught me how a heart speaks. Thanks to him, I can deduce each clap and echo, read meaning in muscle. Much as I love machines, this is one instance in which I prefer to listen for myself – especially if I am listening to him.

'Hmm.' He smiled distantly as he turned my question over. He opened his mouth, closed it in thought, and opened it again. 'I never really liked coffee.'

'Caffeine, or the taste?'

'The taste. But – huh. I suppose I do miss it.'

I rolled up his sleeve. 'Why?'

He looked toward the ceiling, losing himself in a memory as I drew his blood. 'I miss my father making it in the mornings when I lived at home. Everybody else drank it – my mother, my brothers. I don't miss *drinking* it. I miss it being around. I miss the sorts of gatherings that call for coffee.' He was quiet for a moment, then glanced at the monitor I'd plugged his sample into. 'All good?'

I waited as the computer brought up his baseline profile for comparison. Every body is different, and can only be measured against itself. All of our patches and nutrient drips are tailor-made for our individual needs. I, for example, was born red-green colour-blind, and had gene therapy when I was four to give me full trichromatic sight. Elena has an inherited predisposition toward breast cancer, which her patches suppress. Jack's patches perform double-duty as well, providing him with the testosterone he's received since his – as he calls it – second puberty. Chikondi's the only one of us whose medical needs can be described as utterly typical.

'Your exams are so boring,' I said. 'I wish you'd get a vitamin deficiency or something, so I'd have something to write up.'

'I could break my ankle again,' he said, 'if you're that bored.'

I laughed, remembering the enormous pain in the ass that had been Chikondi's fractured malleolus during a two-week-long desert survival training in the Badain Jaran. 'Let's not,' I said. I rolled his sleeve back down, taking care as the fabric passed over his patch. They can fix a lot of things, those synthetic skins, but bone injuries aren't one of them. I'm not a fan of maladies over which we have no control.

'And you?' he said. 'Coffee?'

I thought for a moment about the question I'd thought to ask but not answer. 'I'm fine without,' I said. 'But I already miss the smell.'

The hour was late as we finished our prep work inside, and despite having recently been unconscious for nearly three decades, we were tired. Our side of Aecor had turned away from the sun, and despite our distance, the absence of that one faint light made a difference. It was time to call it a day.

We gathered in the rec room to watch the news bundle OCA had sent us. We sat around the monitor with water and sprouts in lieu of popcorn and beer. The video file was queued. The speakers hummed softly as they waited for input. They waited. And waited. And waited.

Nobody made any motion to play the file. The screen stayed dark.

Jack cleared his throat after a moment. 'It's gonna be weird as shit,' he said loudly.

Chikondi chuckled. I exhaled, glad somebody had said what we were all feeling. Elena smiled her funny smile, reached for the control panel, and pressed play.

I had tried, in advance, to anticipate all the paradigms that could've changed in twenty-eight years. I'd played horrors in my head over and over, knowing that progress is somewhat circular, and the news is rarely a good time.

What I hadn't anticipated was a weird haircut. The young man on screen smiled at the camera, and I'm sure in his mind and in the minds of everyone else who had put the video together, he looked presentable, professional. But I didn't know his haircut, and the shape of his shirt was strikingly odd, and the small bubbled jewellery he wore around his wrists was a look I'd never seen before. I had thought to steel myself for the march of history. I'd neglected to factor in fashion.

It hit me, in that moment, just how far we were from the Earth we'd left.

'Hello, Lawki 6,' he said brightly. I squinted. He sounded North American, but I couldn't quite place him. A desert kid, maybe, from down near the Cascadia-Pacific Republic border. 'My name's Amado Guinto, and I'm a communications specialist here at my hometown campus of OCA PNW.'

My jaw dropped. He was from my neck of the woods. Two hours from where I'd grown up, and he sounded like someone from way down south. I was keen to know where the change had come from – migration? Pop culture? – but no one had thought to answer that, or the question of the cut of his shirt. Our new friend Amado wasn't here to talk about linguistic drift or the influences in aesthetics. He was here to deliver The News: politics, headlines, big names. You know. The important stuff.

The thing about the important stuff is, it's never uplifting. That much, at least, hadn't changed at all. We watched in silence, like students in a depressing lecture, as Amado marched us efficiently through the decades. There were good things in there, wonderful things. We'd eradicated malaria, finally. We'd successfully reintroduced tigers into the wild. We'd made a bus-sized battery that could power a city block for ten years. But the rest of it was an odd mix of unpredictable changes that followed tragically predictable patterns. Wars, elections, lines drawn in the sand. The perpetual ebb and flow of some countries reaching out while others walled themselves in. A constant parade of societal drama, powerful within its own sphere, yet impotent when pitted against the colossal rhythms of the planet itself.

'Storm seasons in all corners of the globe have continued to worsen,' Amado said neutrally, 'with more and more coastal cities pulling back or speeding up development of technological solutions.' His neutrality shifted into polite sympathy. 'Mission specialist Quesada-Cruz, this next portion of the compendium may be difficult for you. I want to say personally that I am sorry to deliver this news.'

We all turned to look at Elena. She'd begun the viewing relaxed in her chair, an arm draped unconcerned over the side. Now she was leaning forward, her face calm while her body braced hard. My eyes flicked from her to the screen, back and forth, back and forth, trying to follow both the facts and her reaction. Images of ruined coastlines and broken levies gave way to an animated map, which, as Amado helpfully explained, showed the spread of catastrophic damage. I pulled my lips inward and pressed them painfully together as the red zone filled the entirety of the land bordering the Gulf of Mexico. Hundreds of cities had been abandoned or flooded beyond repair. To us, one little dot stood out among the rest: Tampico. Elena's hometown.

She got up and left the room.

'Elena,' Jack said.

We heard nothing in reply but the sound of a ladder being climbed, downward.

Chikondi reached for the monitor controls. 'We should—'

Jack halted him. 'Let her be,' he said. 'We're here when she needs us.' He exhaled heavily. 'We're all going to have moments like that, I'm sure.'

The OCA reporter, as if he'd known we'd need it, abruptly shifted tack. 'You should know that everybody here at OCA and across Planet Earth are cheering for you, every step of the way. We're ending this transmission with a present of sorts, sent in by your supporters all over the world. Best of luck, Lawki 6. We can't wait to hear from you.'

The broadcast ended with a montage of homemade messages recorded by OCA supporters, greeting and cheering us on from their living rooms. There were kids, dogs, hand-painted signs, languages and global flavour galore. It was lovely, and hugely appreciated, but the person who'd needed to see it most hadn't.

'I'll play it for her later,' Chikondi said, bookmarking the timestamp where the segment had begun.

I got up and headed for the ladder. Yes, Elena knew we were there for her. In those kinds of situations, though, sometimes it's good to provide a reminder.

Her TEVA suit was missing in the cargo hold; she'd gone outside. I suited up and followed.

Elena wasn't far from the *Merian* – just a short walk away. The ice below her was smooth and flat as the surface of a frozen lake. Around us, though, at a short distance, a wall of jagged pillars spiked upward.

'Hey,' I said.

Elena didn't reply. The lamps on her helmet illuminated her glittering face in the dark, like the icon of a saint. Her expression was impossible to read. She wasn't crying. She wasn't angry. She was just . . . looking.

'*That's* what's different,' she said at last. There was relief behind her words, the satisfaction of an itching problem solved.

'What is?' I asked.

She nodded at the daggers of ice, her headlamps changing their smooth surface from black to white. 'It's so clean.' I didn't understand, and my face must have said so, because she added: 'Ever seen an iceberg flip?'

'No,' I said.

'How about a glacier?'

'A glacier . . . flip?'

Her eyes gave me one brief, chiding flick. 'No, just a glacier, in general.'

The image was conjured, and her point was made. I pictured those oh-so-rare mountains of ice back home, with their dramatic streaks of grey and black that sometimes crowded out the whiteness entirely. The sort of large-scale ice humans are most likely to see on Earth is the ice that forms on land, and by nature, that ice is grubby. Even icebergs, which you might think are washed clean by the waves that cradle them, are marred with the remnants of rocky beaches, sandy canyons, dusty winds that have been etching away mountains for centuries. But there was no sand, nor rock, nor dust on the surface of Aecor. The frosty spires around us weren't ice-covered peaks, but simply ice – the purest sea ice, the kind of thing you'd only find in the heart of polar seas back home, far from the grime of shore. Aecor had no shores, no foundation except for that of the ocean floor. We stood upon water, and nothing but.

'Poor Jack,' she said.

I laughed. 'Poor Jack.' I looked at her. 'Elena, I'm so—'

She grabbed my arm. 'Oh, my God.'

Adrenaline shot through me. 'What?'

'Turn off your lights.' I did. She did. '*Look,*' she said, pointing.

For a moment, there was nothing. My eyes hurried to conform to the darkness, trying to parse the edge between black sky and black ice. But before they could, something else appeared, about a meter ahead of us.

Red. A small patch of soft, fluorescent red, shining quietly up through a hazy pane of ice.

It moved.

I should note that autonomous movement detectable to the human eye is not a conclusive indicator of life. A rock slipping down a hill is not alive. A river is not alive. Lichen, on the other hand, is very much alive, as is pond scum and the yeast in bread dough, but you won't see any of these pick up and scurry across a room (one would hope). Even so, if you see something wiggle its way forward when nothing else around it is moving, there's not a scientist in the world that wouldn't make an assumption there.

Elena remembered protocol before I did. 'Camera,' she said.

Her voice snapped me into action. 'Camera.' I heard a faint click in my helmet as the onboard recording equipment got to work.

'There's a light in the ice ahead of us,' she said, delivering her words with academic composure. 'We noticed it a few seconds before we began recording. Not sure how long it's been there. Flight engineer O'Neill and I are approaching carefully to take a closer look.'

The ice crunched beneath our boots as we walked. My pulse raced as my brain helpfully supplied images of angler fish and glow-worms, luring in the hypnotised to a toothy end. I imagined the ice splintering, the solid surface destroyed as a monstrous alien maw rose up and swallowed us whole and screaming. But Elena walked steady, and so I walked steady, wearing her bravery as my own.

To my relief (and perhaps surprise), there was no splintering, no swallowing. What there was was light – more light, another and another and another. We could tell their sources were bright, and I'm sure if we'd seen them in clear water, their silhouettes would've been crisp and precise. But the ice muted the light, blurring its edges, scattering it in hazy auras that shimmered well beyond the source. New colours joined the party – orange, pink – and new shapes as well. There were snake-like things, full-bodied things, worms and flowers and combs. Some shoaled by the dozens. Some travelled alone. Some bobbed. Some chased. The ice sheet below us became a luminescent symphony, and Elena stopped narrating for the camera. I understood why. None of our words in the moment were good enough. Imagine a summer carnival behind a wintered windowpane. Imagine the most fabulous aurora you've ever seen, shining below your feet.

Elena and I laughed. I grabbed her hand. She pulled me in, her arm wrapped snugly around my shoulders, the top of my helmet resting against the bottom of hers. We were one being, one moment, all boundary of body and person dissolved in the presence of shared euphoria. We stood like children, pointing and gasping. I forgot why she'd gone out onto the ice. It seemed she had as well.

I heard the faint rush of the airlock behind us, followed by a clatter down the ramp and a burst of running. Chikondi – undoubtedly having seen the feeds of our cameras pop up on the monitor – came barrelling toward us, a man on fire. Jack came out of the airlock a few seconds later, running for a few steps, stopping to fix the boot he'd hastily shoved himself into, then continuing onward.

Chikondi was beside himself. The dance of light was in full force now, and he turned this way and that, crying out wordlessly. He took a deep breath, and shouted in crescendo: 'Multi . . . cellular . . . ORGANISMS!' He raised his face to the sky, thrusting his gloved fists in the air like he'd just scored a championship goal.

'Holy shit.' Jack laughed. He put his palms on the top of his helmet. 'Holy *shit*.' He looked at me and Elena. 'Are you still recording?'

'Yes,' Elena said. 'Every word you say.'

'Oh. Well.' Jack walked over to her and turned his gaze straight into her camera lens. 'Holy shit.'

Chikondi wasted no time in training his flock of camera traps on the ice. For ten days, the little machines recorded the glowing soirees taking place in the water below. We did plenty of work in the meantime, harvesting vegetables in the greenhouse, doing routine inspections of the *Merian*'s systems, studying the orbital imagery the cubesats sent back every day. We began environmental studies as well, at Elena's lead. She was in her element atop a frozen sea, where there were ice cores to pull and wind speeds to measure and scrapings to melt down on microscope slides. She worked with laser focus, efficient as ever.

She said nothing of Tampico. The rest of us decided not to ask.

We were her lab techs during this time, and happily so. No astronaut is a pure specialist, and no scientist works alone. To survey an ecosystem, you need to have a base understanding of all its factors. A biologist cannot draw conclusions without knowing how the oceans move and what the air is like. A meteorologist cannot study the composition of the atmosphere without knowing what's breathing into it. And me – I may be the engineer, but not only are my hands as good with a Petri dish as anyone else's, but it helps me to know what my tools are being used for. I *want* to know. If each of us retreated into our own private dens of specialisation, we'd be shooting ourselves in the foot. We benefit from knowing what the other is doing – even Jack, who complained every day about the lack of rocks.

'I would do *anything* for a handful of dirt,' he'd moan. 'Just a spoonful. A crumb.' He'd sigh dramatically at every sparkling ice core we dissected, but it was all in jest. Anytime something new was brought into the clean lab, his eyes lit up as much as anyone's.

At the end of Chikondi's first period of photography, we gathered at his request in the data lab. The three of us sat around the table, tablets and attention at the ready.

Chikondi stood at the sketch board, hands full of styluses, his whole body about to burst with excitement. 'Draw anything you haven't seen before up here on the board, and call it out when you do, so we don't end up "discovering" the same thing twice. Now, at first, *everything's* going to be something we haven't seen before, so we'll begin with reviewing images as a group until we start getting familiar with the phenotypes that are out there. Okay?'

Jack looked at me. 'Can you draw for me? I'm shit at drawing.'

'No,' I said.

'Elena, would you—'

Elena's expression answered his question beyond a shadow of a doubt.

'So long as it's got the right number of legs and an approximate body shape, you'll be fine,' Chikondi said.

'But it's for posterity.' Jack gestured in protest at the sketch board, which would digitally record, archive, and transmit everything we scribbled on it. 'I don't want the history books to say, "This is Jack Vo, trailblazer, Renaissance man, but ultimately, tragically, shit at drawing."'

Elena gave him a look. 'You're being an infant.'

Jack wrinkled his nose at her. '*You're* being an infant.'

Chikondi handed Jack the first stylus. He passed styluses to me and Elena as well, then set down the remaining fistful on one of the lab benches.

'Why did you grab so many?' Elena asked.

'Well, just in case one breaks,' Chikondi said. 'We're going to be here for a while.' He tapped his tablet, syncing his screen to the larger display next to the sketch board, then settled into one of the lab chairs. 'Okay, get ready, everyone. Day one, image one.'

We leaned forward.

Standing on the ice and watching the life forms in motion had been mesmerising. Seeing a snapshot of said same – a dozen or so glowing creatures frozen in time, their forms finally still enough for us to bloodlessly dissect – made us pine.

Jack leapt to his feet, artistic insecurities no match for the siren's call of raw data. 'Put a grid on it.'

Chikondi tapped his screen, and a neat net of squares appeared over the image. He got up, too, his rest in the chair short-lived. He looked electric, like if you touched him you'd feel a snap. 'Okay, okay, ah – first row, first column—'

Jack nodded and began to draw. 'AnA, yeah?' By this, he meant Annelid Approximate, one of OCA's many official classifications. You don't want to call an alien creature a *fish* or a *spider* in a field research context. It may look like an animal back home, and may even *behave* like an animal back home, but it's not the same thing, and shoving everything we find out here into the categories we have on Earth is a dangerous trap. You have to give some kind of name to the things you find, though, and as taxonomy is the sort of long-game activity best done back home, we survey teams use simple acronyms based on terrestrial phyla, to help us visually sort things until proper classification can be determined. So, because it's not very fancy to say 'worm-like,' we say Annelid (e.g. earthworm) Approximate: AnA. You can find this acronym on the same list as Avian Reptile Approximate (AvA), Amphibian Approximate (AA), Mammal Approximate (MA), and so on – plus the ever-exciting 'NP' for 'New Phyla'. Everybody wants to find an NP.

Chikondi got blindingly close to the monitor as he weighed Jack's assessment of the creature in the top left grid. He thought for a minute, then shook his head. 'It's not segmented, it's smooth. And stocky. I say CA.' Cnidarian Approximate, the phyla that includes sea cucumbers.

'Hold on.' Elena joined the fray. 'It's got feet.'

'Where?' Chikondi asked.

Elena pointed at a different grid. 'This is the same species, right?' She made a pulling motion on the monitor, zooming in. 'Look. Isn't that a foot?'

I got up to look, too. We all squinted at the tiny blobs sticking out of the larger blob.

'Hard to say,' Jack said.

'It's in motion,' I said. 'We need a clearer image.'

'I swear that's a foot,' Elena said. 'Or a digit of some kind.'

'Cnidarians have feet, so CA would still be accurate,' Chikondi said. 'Although . . .' He shook his head with the kind of frustrated puzzlement every scientist longs for. He zoomed in closer and frowned. 'Does it have *bones*?'

We leaned even further forward with cartoonish synchrony. We looked, and we looked, and we looked, the pixels somehow becoming less clear with each second that went by.

'Mark it as inconclusive until we see more specimens,' Chikondi said to Jack.

Jack began to write on the sketch board below his drawing of the creature.

Elena looked at Jack's handiwork. 'You really are shit at drawing.'

He casually gave her the finger with his free hand as he wrote: *CA0001 (incon.)*.

So it went for two hours, until all fuel for categorical bickering had been spent. A menagerie of crudely sketched body types filled the board – thirteen suspected new species in total. Thirteen unique animals with their own lives and stories to tell. Thirteen things no human before us had ever seen.

The camera trap is one of the most humane inventions in the ecological survey toolbox, and it excels when paired with its best friend, image recognition software. In the old days, scientists had to manually review every image they took of a jungle road or a wildlife corridor, painstakingly tagging each file with whether it contained elephants or bears or whatever biological quarry they were after. It took a tremendous number of work hours, and often had to be completed by volunteers, simply because there was never enough funding to actually pay the number of people such a task would require. Software that could do the work in a fraction of the time was a godsend, and its development revolutionised the field. There's only one problem with that approach: you have to teach the software what to look for. If you're dealing with creatures nobody's ever seen, you *can't* do that, not at first. The only way forward is old school.

'Okay,' Chikondi said energetically, tapping his tablet. 'On to day one, image two.'

'How much time lapsed between each photo capture?' Jack asked.

'Two minutes,' Chikondi said.

Jack exhaled and cracked his neck. I clapped him on the shoulder in solidarity. Elena smiled silently and folded her arms, looking ready – no, *eager* to forgo sleep for this. She was made for this work. We all were.

A scholar could review the reports we made on Aecor in days, maybe weeks. For the layman, our discoveries can be summed up as follows:

We found an animal with a previously unknown method of propulsion: *Tubuspiscis quesadae*, which looks like a sport sock with the entire toe cut out, if that sock were made of the flesh of a jellyfish instead of fabric. It squeezes the sides of its hollow body to propel itself through the water, gathering nutrients in the dense fur of filters that coats its inner side.

We found no large animals on Aecor during the extent of our survey. This does not mean they do not exist, but we found no supporting evidence that they do. The largest organism we found is *Doliopiscis aecorii*, a fish-approximate species that can reach about half a meter in length. We surmise that Aecor's challenging aquatic environment has hindered the evolution of larger creatures.

We found that much of the life on Aecor is nocturnal. Why this matters at such a great distance from the sun and beneath an ice cap, we don't know. (Chikondi is still stuck on – and agitated by – this puzzle.)

We found enormous mats of an algae-like organism (*Pigertapete aecorii*) that ride the convection currents in a predictable circuit. A host of animals cling to these mats as a means of rather sedentary migration.

We estimate, from the ice cores, that Aecor's surface replaces itself at a regular rate every six thousand years. An impact event appears to have interrupted this cycle some two thousand years ago. Determining the ecological effects of this would require greater study. Based on satellite data, we believe this impact occurred near the Jemison Peninsula, in the southern hemisphere.

We catalogued nine hundred and twenty-six species of multicellular organisms, including thirty-two we happily classified as NP. We additionally catalogued over three thousand species of bacteria. These are not final numbers, by any stretch of the imagination.

Based on our findings, we recommended Aecor as a future site for long-term, dedicated ecological study.

It's staggering to see these things written out like that, because in reality, those seven short summaries represent four Earth years spent on that little moon. Science, you see, is boring. I don't mean *discovery*, and I don't mean *knowledge*. I mean the activity of science – the process, the procedure. That list above can only be written thanks to four years of ice cores, of photo captures, of wind logs, of melt measurements, of databases, of arguments, of launches and landings, of packing and unpacking and repacking the lab, of washing pipettes and stacking slides and decontaminating gloves and goggles exactly the same way every single time. The work is tedious. It is slow. It is not for everyone, even though the end results are.

I took solace in that work, monotonous as it was. The *Merian* ran so beautifully on Aecor that I had little to do for her beyond standard maintenance. I spent most of my time in the lab, helping to process brine samples and program image recognition software (which yes, we were able to use, after about a year). Any task that needed an extra pair of hands, I was there for.

I remember one night in particular, when we were stationed in the place we nicknamed the Misty Plateau. It was late, and the lighting of the *Merian*'s interior wrapped us in warm contrast against the pitch-black beyond the windows. Geysers burst outside at a safe distance, a scattered bouquet of them spreading out across a frigid plain. There was always one going off – sometimes two or three at once, their boiling water hissing loud enough against the stubborn ice for us to hear it through the hull. But there was nothing threatening about the sound. It was a wave crashing, a wind blowing, a geothermic lullaby. I was alone in the clean lab, but I knew where the others were. Elena and Jack were in the data lab, in the throes of a passionate dispute about the nature of the moon's core (I am sure they both relished every second of it). Chikondi was in the greenhouse, tending his leafy crop with care. And there I was, washing Petri dishes – the most mundane, new-kid-in-the-lab chore there is. I stood there, scraping out stubborn growth medium with my gloved fingernail, and I was happy. Content like I could never remember being. I was surrounded by people I loved, safe in a place free of noise and performance and the empty trappings of civilisation. Here, nobody cared about status or money, who was in power, who was kissing or killing whom. There was only water, and the wonders living within it. The right things mattered on Aecor. I'm a secular woman, but that moon felt to me like a sacred place. A monastic world that repaid hard work and dogged patience with the finest of rewards: Quiet. Beauty. Understanding.

'I want to stay here,' I said to Elena one night as we lay nose to nose in her cabin. 'If they'd sent us here just for this, that'd be enough.' Her face shimmered, and I imagined the light waves bouncing from the reflectin in her skin to the reflectin in mine, then back to hers, then back to mine, an endless reciprocity.

'Mmm,' she said. She thought for a moment, stroking my cheek with her thumb. Something shifted in her, and she smiled. 'But think about what we get to do next.'

Mirabilis

The glitter was gone from my skin, but something new had rooted itself beneath. Remember: the human body evolved for Earth gravity and Earth gravity alone, and its internal structure has adapted for that specific force. Just as too much time in microgravity can pose problems without supplementation, so it goes in the opposite direction. Mirabilis is what we call a 'superearth' – a rocky giant nearly double the size of our home-world. On its surface, my body's weight would double (even though my mass would not). So, too, would the weight of everything I needed to lift – crates, tools, toothbrushes, the clothes on my back. Even in the best of shape, the strain would chip away at me if I were unaided. Tears and fractures and stress injuries galore, plus the very real, very frightening likelihood that my circulatory system would eventually give up the laborious task of pushing blood to my brain. That wouldn't be particularly conducive for mission success.

So for Mirabilis, I'd been given extra muscle fibre. Lots and lots of extra muscle fibre.

I am well aware that we *Homo sapiens* are great apes. Even if gene sequencing hadn't proved that fact long ago, it's evident in everything from our grasping hands to our lanky limbs to our fat, omnivorous skulls. There's an anecdote about Queen Victoria visiting the London Zoo and becoming repulsed at the obvious familial resemblance of an orangutan ('frightfully, and painfully, and disagreeably human' was her verdict). But I'm sure she went back to her gilded palace full of tea and paintings and whatnot after that, thus assuring herself of her God-given degrees of separation. Even today, while we largely view our forest-dwelling cousins with far more affection and respect, we like to think we're immeasurably different from them. After all, don't we wear clothes and build houses and talk at length about how very smart we are for understanding that we're apes?

When I looked at the body OCA had given me for Mirabilis, the real difference was made plain: human beings are the runts of the ape litter. We're scrawny. We're sickly. You'd need to be a champion weightlifter to get within spitting distance of the strength possessed by the most wilting gorilla. Perhaps you've seen an ape in a zoo – a chimpanzee, let's say – and noted, as they shimmy up two-storey ropes with the ease of strolling through a park, how ludicrously ripped they are.

Trust me when I say you can't begin to understand muscles like that until your body is made of them.

I've been in 2Gs for brief periods countless times over – launches, landings, sharp turns in training planes. It's a squeeze, a pressure. Like being underwater, but without the benefit of buoyancy. That feeling still existed on Mirabilis, but thanks to somaforming, I had the means to work within it. I'm sure you've heard the phrase 'survival of the fittest'. It's often misused, operating on the false interpretation that *fit* means *physically fit*, therefore expressing a dog-eat-dog ethos. The strongest wins the day. But that's not what Darwin meant, not at all. He meant *most suited to*, as in, the creatures most suited to – or *most fit for* – a specific environment are the ones with the best chance of passing on their genes. A sloth is fit for a slow life in the branches. A worm is fit for chomping decaying leaves in the damp dark. A tick is fit for patiently waiting on a blade of grass, waiting for a sanguineous passerby to drink from.

By the same token, I was fit for life on Mirabilis. The fact that I was *also* physically fit was just a nice bit of synchrony

– not to mention novelty, in my case. I know what it is to be smart. I know what it is to be creative. I've never before felt strong, not like that. My body was powerful. My limbs were stocky. My thickened heart thudded boldly, a drumbeat deep and hale. My bones had likewise been altered for the task, dense enough to provide a more reliable framework. I wasn't some sort of demigod or fairy-tale hero. I was simply me, reinforced.

I couldn't wait to see what I could do with that.

I want you to picture the following creatures: a bat, a bird, and a bee. Specifically, picture their wings. All of these limbs serve the same purpose, but structurally, they're quite different. Their wings, to put it simply, are not related to each other. In biology, this is called *convergent evolution* – two or more species independently developing similar features that weren't present in their most recent common ancestor. Bats and bees can both fly, but this doesn't mean they're cousins. These creatures did not branch off from one airborne great-grandparent. Bats have a ground-dwelling lineage, and left their rodent-like family on the ground around fifty million years ago. Bees, on the other hand, are part of a very ancient line of flying insects that dates back to the Carboniferous Period – more than three hundred million years ago. Wildly divergent evolutionary paths, resulting in the same essential means of locomotion.

I find this concept so beautiful.

On Earth, the term *invertebrate* – anything without a spine – covers an astounding variety of body types. Spiders, sea hares, millipedes, cuttlefish, dragonflies, and clams all fit the bill. By comparison, vertebrates – snakes, zebras, condors, you and me – are tediously similar below the skin. The spine evolved only once in Earth history, and every being with a skeleton can trace itself back to the same root. We follow a basic template: a bilateral arrangement of skull, ribs, and pelvis, typically accompanied by four limbs. We have two eyes, one mouth, and a brain.

The inner structure of our limbs is similarly predictable: one large upper bone, two parallel lower bones, the many little bones that form the wrist or ankle, and digits. We're all working off of the same blueprint.

This is not the case on Mirabilis. Our time there was too short to do a full evolutionary study, but from the moment we touched down, it was obvious that life on that world had followed a very different trajectory. From observation alone (and with the mountain of caveats that implies), we hypothesise that on Mirabilis, spine-like structures independently evolved at least three times.

It's impossible to predict, as progeny of Earth, how shocking a thing it is to walk into a tableau of vertebrates sporting different skeletal templates. We think we know what biological diversity is. Imagine standing in a wild place – let's say a riparian meadow in a North American forest. Let's also say that it's late spring, and that you're particularly lucky with the animals who have chosen to cross your path that day. It'd be only natural to marvel at the assortment before you – elk, bears, squirrels, hawks, salmon, salamanders, raccoons, turkeys, maybe even a bobcat. No two alike. Animals with physical differences so stark and overt, they're one of the first things we teach to young children.

And yet, all of those creatures possess two eyes, one mouth, limbs with digits, and so on. They are, at the core, the same.

Jack won the dice roll on Mirabilis. It's fortuitous that we lacked the live video coverage of the Apollo and Eridania missions, because the immortal words that flowed forth from mission specialist Jack Vo's mouth as he became the first human to set foot on this new planet were: 'What the fuck is *that*?'

We left that portion of audio out of our official report.

The worst part is, I can't tell you what the fuck *that* was, in Jack's eyes, because everything before us conjured the same question. I'm struggling to explain to you what we saw as we descended the ladder a few hours after we landed (we had to give the local residents some time to calm down and perhaps forget about the loud fiery thing that had landed in their midst). Every word in my vocabulary uses something from Earth as a reference point, and Mirabilis posed challenges for all of them.

Take, for starters, the ground cover. If I am to be a good scientist, I shouldn't say we landed in *grassland*, because the stuff around our feet was not made of blade-like leaves peeling away from stems, but rather flexible spiralling stalks, each rising up to knee-height in a tight corkscrew (*Spirasurculus oneillae*). We learned later that these autotrophs (organisms that don't need to consume a living source of energy, as animals do) do not photosynthesise at all. They chemosynthesise, like the creatures you find clinging to ocean vents back home. *Spirasurculus* suck the energy and nutrients they need from the groundwater below them. They grow upward not to reach for the sun, but to provide a landing place for a tiny flying creature we dubbed *Murmurus voii*, with which they are symbiotic. But, again, if I were to say we landed in 'a field of curly plants', this would lead you astray, because *Spirasurculus* are *not* plants. Yet 'plant' is the best word I have if I want to paint you a mental picture. *Spiracurculus* would mean nothing to you if I had not explained it, nor would the inaccessibly academic descriptor *monocotoloid chemoautotroph*. If I have to pause at every word to explain what it actually means, most of you would understandably wander off before I'd finished setting the scene.

So, for the moment, let's sacrifice accuracy for the sake of impressionism: we landed in an alien 'grassland', surrounded by spindly 'trees' frocked with black 'leaves' – black, like all plant-approximates on Mirabilis, so as to absorb more of the subtle light. The hills undulated, pillow-like, so rounded they almost looked liquid. The sky was pale orange, an aesthetic I can only describe as 'bright dusk', despite it being midday. Due to the closeness of Mirabilis' orbit, the sun was huge in the sky, yet not blinding. There was an ornamentation of other orbital bodies up there as well: a selection of Mirabilis' seventeen moons, plus its sibling planets Opera and Votum, patiently waiting for us. We had landed in summer, mild and carefree. There were clouds, as an afterthought. There was a breeze, but barely. It was, to our human sensibilities, a perfect day.

The creatures before us seemed to agree.

I noticed their strength first. Everything on Mirabilis is robust, bold, built for heavy Gs and a cool sun. The imposing muscularity of this menagerie struck me immediately. My own supplemented strength felt like a cheap facsimile when faced with the genuine article.

The limbs were what I registered next, of which Mirabilis has three main phenotypes. First, the pairs of three: lumbering spotted behemoths with six pillared legs, and flap-like lips that rolled back in four directions to accommodate entire treetops. Pinch-faced herbivores with two pairs of on-pointe legs for locomotion, plus two intimidating scythe-shaped arms (primarily used for nothing more threatening than the alien equivalent of threshing wheat). Social flocks of tendril-covered fliers, each about the size of a skunk, held aloft by six wings that folded efficiently back whenever they left the air to wriggle through pondwater.

Next, the pairs of seven (seven!): a fleet-footed arboreal climber with long silky fur and a face like the ghost of a greyhound, breathtaking in its oddness and shocking in its beauty. A small group of split-snouted, hog-like scavengers in the midst of a violent argument over a fruiting shrub. A solitary smooth-skinned thing that has no Earthly equivalent, which everything else was avoiding or shouting at. It shivered through the shadows, watching the hog-bodies intensely but never making a move. It did not open its mouth, as we stood there, but I was afraid of whatever it held within.

And finally, the single pairs, the most unexpectedly unsettling of the lot. Bipedalism is not a common trait on Planet Earth, and typically we associate it either with ourselves – and thus an unfounded indicator of intelligence – or birds, which are physically so unlike us in every other way that we often forget we both walk in roughly the same manner. But though birds are without arms, they still have four limbs. When you look at the skeletal wings of a bird, you can see the shoulders, the wrist, the phalanges. You understand that the template is the same as ours. Not so with the trio of bipedal creatures we found at the first Mirabilis landing site. They had legs, which attached to a stump of a torso, which in turn attached (without any approximation of a neck) to something akin to a head, except it had no orifices beyond a sucking tube. A thick fringe of hairy feelers was its only guide to the plants it absent-mindedly drained, bumbling clumsily from one feeding spot to the next in a manner that felt like a pointed insult toward everyone who had ever assumed 'two legs' means 'smart'.

We had known there was life on Mirabilis. The atmospheric data gathered by OCA were indicative of virtually nothing else. We had *not* known said life would be anything like this. This was a jackpot, an offering so absurdly rich it almost seemed as if the planet was pulling a prank. Have you ever seen one of those dinosaur paintings from the 1800s, in which the artist crammed every known Jurassic species onto a single teeming riverbank? That was what lay before us, only the artist's palette was robbed of green and blue, and every assumption of vertebrate evolution had been thrown out the window.

'Camera!' we each commanded, nearly in unison. Elena looked ravenous. Jack kept muttering 'wow' again and again, punctuated with reflexive swearing. Chikondi wept silently. But I can't say what I felt in that moment, any more than I can properly call *Spirasurculus* a grass. As an astronaut, you know conceptually that you're going to another world, that you're going to see alien life. You know this, and yet there is nothing that can prepare you for it. It's going to the zoo and seeing an animal you've never heard of. It's seeing footage of a deep sea jelly whose body shape makes you feel as though you're going mad. It's the uncanny valley, pumped full of breath and blood. That first moment on Mirabilis rendered me a child – not joyous, like we'd been on Aecor with our glowing swimmers, but overwhelmed. A toddler surrounded by the knees and noise of adults, tasked with learning the entire world from scratch.

That said, the joy was quick to follow.

'I've got the news downloaded, whenever you're ready.'

If Chikondi registered what I'd said, he didn't show it. His camera traps had been chugging along for a few hours, but he couldn't wait. He was in the data lab, going frame by frame through his helmet recordings from landing – playing a little, pausing the video, drawing what he saw, repeat. It was a tedious way to review material. He didn't care in the slightest. He was drawing in a frenzy, scribbling limbs and notes so furiously that his normally tidy handwriting was nearly illegible.

'Hey. Chikondi,' I said.

He looked up at last, surprised. He hadn't even heard me walk up.

'Want to watch the news?'

'Oh. Um.' Chikondi blinked, thrown off track. He thought for a moment, then pointed at the video monitor. 'Can I—'

I nodded easily. 'Yeah, sure. No rush. Do your thing.'

He threw himself back into it, drawing with gusto.

I went looking for the others. Elena was in the control room, tinkering with a digital thermometer. The entire table was filled with meteorological gear, lined up in neat rows.

'Something wrong with it?' I asked, ready to fetch a toolbox.

She didn't look up, but she heard me. 'No, no,' she said. 'Just making sure everything works for tomorrow.'

'I already ran diagnostics on everything,' I said.

'I know,' she said. 'Just double-checking.' She continued sorting.

I knew her well enough to not take this as an insult, but it needled me a bit all the same. 'Do you want to watch the news?'

Elena needed no time to consider this. She shook her head. 'I'll watch it later,' she said. She looked up at me and gave me a short smile – the sort of smile that says *you're not annoying me, and I appreciate you, but leave me alone so I can work*. So I did.

It wasn't hard to find Jack. I could hear him huffing and puffing across the corridor as he hit the exercise equipment hard.

'Hey,' he exhaled. His cheeks were flushing fire, and rivers ran down his temples. 'This sucks in double-G.' He grinned as he said the words. The challenge delighted him.

'Looks it,' I said. I watched him heave himself back and forth on the rowing machine, beads of sweat flinging from his freshly shorn scalp. 'You do know we've got plenty of fieldwork ahead.'

'Yeah.' One rep.

'And walking.'

'Yeah.' Another rep.

I paused, waiting for him to acknowledge that a normal work day would give him all the exercise he needed. He did not. I shrugged. 'I've got the news downloaded.'

'Okay,' he said. Two reps. Three reps. Four.

'Do you want to watch?'

Five. Six. Seven. Eight. He stopped, panting hard, and reached for his water bottle. 'Nah,' he said.

'Just . . . not at all?'

'Not right now, anyway,' he said.

'Why?'

He took a gulp of water and mopped his brow with his shirt. 'I saw things today I've never imagined. *Could* never have imagined. Things were good, on Aecor, but *this*—' There was an awed look in his eyes, a boy standing in a dream. 'I mean, God.' He laughed, words falling short.

'I know,' I said, and I did, I truly did. 'But the news—'

'Doesn't matter,' he said simply.

I frowned. 'Yes, it does.'

'Why?' he asked. 'It's over a decade out of date. It doesn't affect us, and there's nothing we can do to change any of it. We know what our mission is. We know how to do our jobs. Why should we distract ourselves from that? Especially when the distraction sucks.'

'But we— they—' I disagreed with him, but I felt like I was standing on shaky ground. 'The news is what's happening to the people who sent us here. We should care about that.'

'Of course we care. We wouldn't be doing this job if we didn't care. But our work is how we contribute. Listen, every time we watch the news, the air in here gets heavy for a few days. Or longer. It eats at us. Why are we letting something millions of kilometres away and fourteen years behind fuck up our ability to focus on the thing we were actually sent here to do?' He finished his water. 'If there's something important, we'll get a mission update. But the news – I mean, how does it help me to know that some fuckwit I've never heard of is leading a coup, or whatever? It doesn't. So, that's how we show we care – by doing a good job. We can catch up on world history anytime we want to. Because it *is* history by now. We don't need to know every shred of political bullshit that'll happen over the next decades in order to fit in once we get back. Nobody on *Earth* stays that up-and-up. Why do we have to?'

I didn't know what to say to that. Something in it didn't sit right, but I could find no argument. I didn't want to watch the news either, not really. Maybe Jack was right. Why should I fill my head with something I couldn't change? What was a war on Earth to us? What was an economy to us? To the creatures outside? To the spiralling plants? Nothing around me changed if I chose to not watch the news, but something within me always did. I thought of my crew, each doing in that moment exactly what they wanted to be doing. That seemed like a much saner way to be. I remained unsure, but I nodded.

Jack smiled, stood, and kissed me on the cheek. 'I'm gonna go shower,' he said.

'Please, please do,' I said, wrinkling my nose.

He gave me a smug look – one that said he knew he was a mess, and that he knew something else, too. 'Wanna come with?'

I did.

None of us watched the news that day.

None of us watched the news for four years.

I had thought that our time on Mirabilis would feel slow, that it would drag along with our bodies against the pull of the ground. But my memories of that world are a blur – no, blur's not the right word. I remember it all, distinct and clear. A flip-book, then. A thousand distinct images, rushing past my eyes so fast they take on a life of their own.

Images like: waking in the data lab, sleeve lines pressed deep into my cheek, neck creaking as I raised my head from the table, Chikondi asleep across two chairs beneath a sketch board over-flowing with tapestries of thought about legs and lungs and trophic structure. His headphones were hanging around his neck, and I could hear music flowing tinnily. I thought about waking him, but I knew he hadn't slept the night before that, either. He was a phoenix, burned to ash for the moment, resting in antici-pation of the next spark. I turned off his headphones, covered him with my jacket, and tiptoed out.

Like: following Elena in the dawning hours to collect water from the fog fences down at the Al-Ijliya shoreline. An animal had damaged the netting at one site, too vigorous in its sucking of the condensed salt. The unexpected damage frustrated her; I fixed it on the spot. She told me when we got home that she missed when my hair was long enough to pull, then let me sit with that thought as she disappeared behind a microscope for the rest of the day. I fell asleep that night with her curled around my back like a protective shell. I knew she was still pondering the fragile things that live in clouds, and it made me press my spine against her all the harder.

Like: Jack hooking his gloved fingers through my toolbelt loop and tugging me out the airlock, me catching the shovel he tossed through the air, us digging down, down, down to where the living soil turned into slippery clay that wept warm and wet when pressed between our palms. Water began to pool around our feet, and we climbed back into the sun with our samples, racing to see whose strapping arms could ferry them the faster. We tied. We laughed.

Like: Chikondi waking me after midnight with an apology and a grin and the news that he'd finally, finally figured out where *Comusporcus dakaii* laid its eggs.

Like: Elena standing against a sunset, watching gliding hunters coast on thermals, dropping into dizzying dives after their airborne prey.

Like: Jack whistling as he straddled a boulder to unearth an embedded skull, cleaning out its fossilised eye sockets with a dental pick.

Like: early mornings, late nights, failed naps, wild dreams, quarrels, epiphanies, shouted answers, excited questions, hands that ached from work, eyes that burned from staying open, bruises that made me smile, thoughts that raced and never slowed.

People say things like 'if we'd found only one new species, it would've been enough'. I said something very like it on Aecor. Nothing was ever enough on Mirabilis. Every discovery made, every hour spent in someone else's sheets, every conversation and collaboration and new vista taken in made me want more, more, more. We were alive on that world. We were kings without enemies, children removed from time.

We should've known better, as students of the universe. There's no escaping entropy.

*

To understand what happened, you must first understand decontamination protocol for bringing gear used outside back into the *Merian*.

Step 1: Retrieve all gear from the field. Check meticulously to ensure no items are left behind.

Step 2: Remove any dust, dirt, organic matter, or other visible contaminants using the cleaning kit. (This includes an arsenal of tools for any sort of clean-up, everything from a concentrated air blower to hydrogen peroxide to a handheld UV wand.)

Step 3: Securely latch all boxes, crates, and other storage containers.

Step 4: Proceed into the airlock with your gear. Orient all storage containers so that Side A is facing upward. Activate the airlock's cold plasma system to sterilise storage container exteriors, as well as the exterior of your TEVA suit.

Step 5: After the first sterilisation cycle is complete, orient all containers so that Side B is facing upward. Activate the cold plasma system. During this cycle, sit on the floor in order to expose the soles of your boots.

Step 6: Open each storage container. Activate the cold plasma system to sterilise your equipment and the container interiors.

Step 7: If any visible contaminants have been discovered during this procedure, clean and sterilise the equipment again. Place any collected contaminants into the incineration chamber.

Step 8: Securely latch all storage containers. Proceed into the spacecraft.

This process is a time-consuming pain, but a vital one. Nothing that originated outside can be allowed within.

All four of us were present in the cargo hold that afternoon, our last day on Mirabilis. I was taking inventory of the storage stacks, ensuring that every crate and strap was where it should be. Jack and Elena were carrying in the last of the equipment from the clean lab (this, too, has its own airlock and plasma chamber). Chikondi was in the 'front door' airlock, placing his camera trap crates on a dolly after the final sterilisation cycle. Through the large window, I could see the last of the plasma ebbing around him, a luminous purple fog retreating into wall vents.

I took a box of lab tools from Jack and slid it into its designated place. We'd been at it for hours, and even with their extra strength, my arms and legs were beginning to protest. 'Hey, anybody want to order pizza after this?' I said.

Elena gave an amused smile as she stacked. 'And beer?'

'Of course beer,' Jack said. 'Who has pizza without beer?'

I checked their items off the list on my tablet. 'Olives and mushrooms?' I asked.

Elena made a face. 'I hate mushrooms.'

'Really?'

'Yes.'

I'd never noticed that, but then, we'd spent far more time eating spacecraft salad together than we had eating normal fare back on Earth. 'Jack?' I asked.

Jack shrugged as he lifted another box. 'Not much of a fungus man, but I'll eat them.'

'Hmm.' I turned my attention to Chikondi, who was coming out of the airlock with the dolly in tow. 'Care to weigh in on the mushroom debate of 2162?'

'They're okay, but why on pizza?' he said. 'Stick to the classics. Cheese, sauce, pepperoni. Why mess with—'

His words ceased as one of his boxes crashed to the floor.

Jack and Elena turned their heads. I frowned; so did Chikondi. The errant object on the floor hadn't fallen from the top of the pile. It had dislodged itself from a middle row. There was only about a second or two to process this before the box jolted itself several centimetres to the right.

Chikondi jumped back.

'The *fuck*,' Jack said.

The box moved again. It kept moving, shuddering this way and that without clear direction.

Elena covered her mouth with her hand.

Chikondi took a breath, then another, then another. Slowly, he inched forward, reaching a hesitant arm out, keeping his body as far from his hand as physically possible. If the source of the movement had been a malfunctioning machine suddenly activating on its own – maybe one of the rotational drivers on a camera trap – it would continue moving at Chikondi's touch. It would buzz against his hand, clatter chaotically out as he got the box open, maybe result in a bandage or two, provide us with a funny story we could tell at speaking engagements down the road about the glitching gadget that gave us all heart attacks.

But fingers touched metal, and the box held still.

There was nothing Chikondi wanted to do less than pick up that box. His face made that fact plain as day. But he crouched down. He picked it up. There was a loud rustle from inside as he did. 'Oh, God,' he moaned.

Elena made it to the emergency panel before I did. She slammed her hand against the big red button labelled *Containment*. The doors to the modules and the upper decks quickly closed. The air filters sealed themselves off, no longer pulling air from the cargo hold. 'Airlock,' she shouted.

Chikondi dashed back to the airlock with the box, as if it were ablaze and a bucket of water was waiting. He hit a button; the door slid shut behind him. The rest of us hurried to the window and watched as Chikondi bent down to the box to unfasten the latch. He swung the lid open and got the hell out of the way.

I pressed as close as I could to the door, trying to get a good look. The glass fogging up wasn't a concern, because for the moment, I'd stopped breathing.

Something about the size of a sock leapt out of the box, arcing away from Chikondi. It scurried to the far edge of the airlock, darting back and forth, trying to find a way out. Its movements were frantic, but bit by bit, I managed to process its shape. Six stout legs. A dainty brush of a split tail. A flat-faced head atop a serpentine body. Delicate, soft-looking quills festooned its back, and the white fur of its sides was peppered with a stunning spray of multi-coloured dots. Gill-like flaps surrounded its snug mouth, and from these it vocalised, letting out a plaintive trill as it tried to escape.

We catalogued nearly ten thousand macroscopic species during our four years on Mirabilis. We'd never seen anything even remotely like this one.

'I don't know,' Chikondi said, answering the question none of us would say aloud. 'I – I don't know how. I checked, I checked the boxes after I got the traps in, I always check—'

'Did you turn your back on an open box?' Elena asked.

'No,' Chikondi said.

'You must've,' she said.

'I – I mean, I – I don't remember doing so—'

'How did you not see this during decon?' Her eyes widened. 'Did you not run plasma on the interiors?'

'Of course I did!'

'He did,' I said. 'I saw. Three cycles.'

'Then how did he miss *that*?' Elena demanded.

'Maybe—' I scrambled for an answer. 'Maybe the – Chikondi, can you see inside the box?'

Chikondi moved tentatively toward the box, and thus toward the animal, but he had nothing to fear from it. The animal was far more afraid of him than the other way around. It wailed and scurried to the opposite end of the airlock. Both of them were breathing heavily as Chikondi checked the box. His head sagged. He lifted the box, showing us the spot where the foam liner had begun to pull away from the side, creating a little pocket. It wasn't much, but something quick and flexible might get curious about such a cosy space.

Chikondi looked haggard. 'I thought – I must have – I could've sworn I—'

Elena rubbed her face and turned away. 'This is why protocol exists.'

'Jesus, Elena,' Jack snapped. 'Look how fucking fast that thing moves.' He turned to Chikondi. 'Could've happened to any of us.'

The animal was in a full panic now, digging with futile frenzy at the seam of the wall.

Chikondi sat down on the floor and held out his palm. 'Shh,' he said to the animal. 'Shh, shh, it's okay, it's okay.'

Elena walked off in search of something.

'It was in the box,' Jack said. 'It was just in the box. He didn't open the box in the cargo hold, it didn't breathe any of our air—'

I shut my eyes. I knew where he was going with this. I wanted to go there, too. 'Those boxes aren't airtight,' I said. 'They're not specimen containers, they're just storage—'

'It was in here for half a minute, if that.'

'And it's in an airlock full of our air now,' I said.

'Plus it went through plasma cycles,' Elena said, returning to the door with a device in hand.

'Shit,' Jack said, shutting his eyes. We all knew what that meant. An airlock plasma cycle isn't like medical plasma treatment, where a light dose is targeted on a patch of infected skin. This was full-body, heavy-duty exposure, never intended for living tissue. Beyond eradicating whatever symbiotic dermal bacteria this animal needed to stay alive in its natural biome, there was no telling what side effects the animal itself might suffer, or what mutations it could carry with it. Release was out of the question.

'Shh, shh,' Chikondi said to the animal. 'Come on, come on, you're going to hurt yourself—' He shook his head at himself. 'I *checked*—' he whispered.

Elena put the device in the equipment drawer and slid it through the wall. 'It's right here,' she said.

Chikondi did not look at her, or the drawer. On his knees, he inched closer to the animal, palm outstretched. 'Come on, it's okay.'

'Chikondi—' Elena said, terse with concern.

He whipped his head toward her, eyes shining with tears. 'I don't want it to die afraid,' he said.

Elena pursed her lips and looked down at the floor. Her disapproval was plain, but she said nothing further. Behind us, Jack paced, hands folded over the back of his neck.

Chikondi closed his eyes and gathered himself. He pulled his palm back and leaned against the wall, folding his legs beneath him, trying to stay calm for the sake of them both. They remained that way for several minutes, the grieving man and the frightened alien. Eventually, the animal's movements slowed down, and though it still searched for an exit, its cries and digging began to ebb.

'Camera,' Chikondi said. His voice was hollow. He took a shaking breath as he began to record. 'Specimen is hexapodal, and both fur and body shape are Mammal Approximate. However, it does not resemble any of the other MA species we have catalogued here. Further study would be needed, but I find it likely this is a new phyla.' He leaned his head back against the wall. 'It's a very beautiful animal.' A few silent seconds passed. 'Stop camera.' He looked through the window at me. 'Ariadne, would you get me an exam kit?'

I did. I dropped it into the drawer, beside the device Elena had deposited: a stun gun. Chikondi retrieved her offering first.

'Do you want me to do it?' Elena asked. 'I can suit up fast.'

'No,' Chikondi said. *Yes*, his voice said. 'I should do it, it's my fault.'

'It's not your fault,' Jack said.

Elena did not second that comment.

The animal ran from Chikondi's approach, but not fast, and not far. It was keeping its distance, but was seemingly in the first stages of understanding that he wasn't a threat. It held still in the corner, turning its face toward him. It rose up on its back legs, sitting like a meerkat, the structures around its mouth rippling steadily. Smelling him, perhaps. Figuring him out. It is impossible to know what it was doing. To assume that it was curious would be pure speculation.

But to me, it felt curious.

'I'm sorry.' The words ripped themselves from Chikondi's throat. 'I'm so sorry.'

We watched through the window as Chikondi raised the gun. I watched him turn it up to a level that would've killed an Earth animal twice its size. He raised the device and pulled the trigger.

The animal screamed. A moment of this was to be expected – an involuntary cry at the end. But it *continued* screaming, and flailing, too, an obscene dance of fear and agony. It hadn't died.

So Chikondi shot it again.

The fur began to smoke, and it screamed.

He shot it again.

Its legs spasmed, and it screamed.

He shot it again.

And still, it screamed. Despite the spittle that leaked from its mouth, despite the charred fur and the splitting blisters beneath, it wouldn't stop screaming.

Jack turned away. Elena swallowed thickly.

Chikondi was shaking by now, the stun gun rattling in his hand. 'I'm sorry!' he cried. 'Please – please just—' He hit it a fifth time. There was a squeal, a shudder.

Finally, the animal was dead.

Chikondi threw the weapon aside and stumbled into the corner opposite the mess we'd never be able to fully scrub from the floor. He propped himself against the wall as he retched miserably inside his helmet.

Elena shut her eyes. 'We'll need to do decon again for all the boxes,' she said. 'Everything that's in here, and ourselves, too.' She sighed. 'I'll write the report.'

'No,' I said. I was angry at her, for no reason other than I needed to be angry and pragmatism was the best target on hand. 'I'll write it.'

The next morning, I awoke alone. My body was stiff and weary after the business of sterilising the contents of the entire cargo hold, and I had no desire to write anything, let alone get up. But I got up. I went to the comms console. I wrote the report. I sent it off.

I glanced at the comms inbox. The number forty-three hovered over the news download folder, indicating all the bundles we'd blissfully ignored. I'd seen it hundreds of times after filing reports, a nagging nuisance out of the corner of my eye. I'd long stopped paying attention to it. It had been there for so long now that it was just background noise, a graphical element. But that day, the number glared at me in accusation. The spell of Mirabilis had been broken, and guilt was seeping in around the seams.

An emergent thought itched. Forty-three. Forty-three. The number bothered me, for no readily available reason. I frowned at the screen for a moment, then finally opened the folder.

Merian news bundle – March 2162, the last file read.

My frown deepened. In Earth time, the date was November 21, 2162. Given the amount of time it took for messages to reach Mirabilis, and given OCA's comms output schedule, the last news bundle would've been sent on November 1. *That's* why forty-three was bothering me. Given the time we'd been on that planet, we were seven bundles short.

The *Merian* hadn't downloaded a news bundle in seven months.

The emergency folder had no number hovering over it – a message received there we never would ignore – but I opened it anyway. Empty. Same for the mission updates folder. Empty. This wasn't unexpected. When we arrived at Mirabilis, Earth would've only just received confirmation of our arrival at Aecor. But given the gap in the news folder, a sinking question arose: were those empty folders simply empty . . . or had something crucial been lost in the ether? If the news wasn't making it to us, what else had gone missing?

Elena walked in from the gym a few minutes after I started running a diagnostic on the comms system. 'What's wrong?' she asked.

I told her. 'I'm checking to make sure we're still receiving signal.'

A frown formed on her face as well, but it was directed at me, not the problem. 'Weren't you running daily diags?'

'Of course I was,' I said, which was part of what bothered me. The comms system had never shown any issues, and yes, I checked it every day. A problem that had arisen over the past twenty-four hours wouldn't account for six months of missed messages.

Elena watched over my shoulder as the diagnostic ran its course, as if I wouldn't tell her the second I had any news. Whether she intended the implication or not, it stung.

The final report appeared. Green lights all around.

Jack entered the room, hair wet from his last shower before the next round of torpor. 'What's up?'

I explained. He didn't like it.

'What if the *diagnostics* are wrong?' Elena asked. 'Could there be a hardware problem?'

'It's unlikely,' I said. 'I spent the whole week doing pre-launch checks.'

'Do you think we should do them again?' she asked. It wasn't really a question.

'Well, hang on,' Jack said. A third frown joined the party. 'What if we don't have anything because they didn't send us anything?'

OCA lived and breathed by mission plans. If they wanted

you to set your wake-up alarm differently, you got a mission update. If they wanted you to change your toothpaste, you got a mission update. News bundles were a scheduled part of our expected communications. If they were going to stop sending them, we'd have received a mission update to that effect. But nothing had appeared in that folder, not once.

'Let's—' Elena began.

'Yeah,' I said, opening the most recent bundle. I glanced around as the file unpacked itself. 'Where's Chikondi?'

'I think he's still in his cabin,' Jack said.

I looked at the clock. It was after ten. That wasn't like Chikondi. 'Should we get him?'

Whatever Jack started to say, it was lost as the video started. There was an OCA logo and an OCA employee in an OCA office . . . but something was off.

'Hello, Lawki 6,' the man on screen said. He cleared his throat. He seemed to be uncomfortable in front of a camera. 'I hope you're all doing great.' His eyes were fixed off to the side; he was reading from a prompt.

'Can you turn it up?' Elena asked.

I checked the volume. 'It's already all the way up,' I said.

'Can barely hear him,' she said. I agreed; the sound quality was mediocre at best. I listened to the man's delivery, and though I had no proof, I was willing to bet that he wasn't a member of the comms team. He felt like a stand-in, the person who'd said *I guess I can do it* after a long silence at a meeting. I started to notice other miniscule oddities as well: the sun-faded fabric of the OCA flag, a small corner of chipped paint on the wall, the heavy jacket the man was wearing indoors. Something wasn't right.

Whatever that something was, the news bundle shed no light on it. All we got was a dizzying melange of conflicts without context, political leaders whose names we didn't know, all-consuming dramas that would likely be forgotten a generation later. Have you ever looked at the headlines on a foreign news site, and felt completely adrift? The experience was like that, but on the scale of the entire planet. The plot escaped us entirely.

'Stay safe out there,' the man said with an awkward wave. 'We'll talk to you next month.'

And that was that.

We three sat silently for a moment, our frowns all the more pronounced.

'Try the one before that,' Jack said.

So we did. We watched another, and when that told us nothing, we jumped back ten months to see if chronological order would help. Chikondi joined us at last, saying little of anything, but present for the puzzle at hand. A few pieces started to fall into place. They only raised more questions.

OCA was experiencing funding problems – we'd gathered that much, even though the bundles did their best to make light of it. Nothing was said of where the shortage in finances was coming from, but the greater context of the stories relayed to us made it plain. There was war. There was famine. There were too many people in cities that already had too many when we'd left. It is difficult to give thought to the stars when the ground is swallowing you up. And if *thought* is difficult, it stands to reason that money is even harder. We watched as the clothes got more and more tired. The faces did, too. But in every bundle, the closing sentiment was the same: *We're proud of you. Stay safe. We'll talk to you next month.*

Until, some nebulous day before April 2162, they stopped. They simply stopped.

We sat in silence around the monitor. We'd screwed up our launch schedule by cramming the news all day, but that no longer seemed like the bigger priority.

Jack shook his head at the screen. He stood. He paced. 'Where are they?' he said. 'Where did they go?'

Opera

I remained in front of the mirror for much longer than I had the two times before. The sun was large in Opera's sky, so I did not need to shine. The gravity was on par with Earth, so I did not need to be strong. There was much about Opera that was like Earth, in fact – its size, its atmosphere, its temperature range. I needed nothing special for Opera, so I was given nothing. My previous gifts were gone, no longer maintained by the patch on my arm. The radiation and antifreeze supplementations remained, of course, but beyond that, I was just . . . me.

Looking in the mirror, I wasn't sure I liked what that equated to. I was almost eleven years older than when I'd left Earth. That's not so much time, but the changes of ageing had largely escaped my notice, distracted as I was by the more dramatic differences of somaforming. I didn't mind the lines in my face, but I also didn't remember their development. My hair hadn't grown too much in the five years spent in torpor, but the frequent shaving meant I never saw it much longer than maybe a centimetre. Now, I saw frequent threads of wintry grey among the black tufts. My body was average, healthy, nothing out of the ordinary. That was the problem. Without the glitter, I felt dull; without the brawn, puny. To my eyes, I looked ill, and the sight made me sink.

I found my crewmates where I'd bid them goodnight, down in the control room, arranged around the comms monitor. Jack shook his head at me as I floated through the door.

'Nothing,' he said.

'Nothing?'

He shook his head again.

'Have you run a—'

'Yes,' Elena said. 'Everything's as it was when we left. All green lights.'

Chikondi floated in the corner, silent in thought and distant in gaze.

'They can't just be *gone*,' I said.

'No,' Jack said in agreement. 'Even if funding ran out entirely, they'd tell us. They wouldn't just say, whoops, oh well, no more paychecks, guess we'll fuck off. No, something's wrong. Something's really wrong.'

'I'll check the comms again,' I said. 'I'll do another full hardware check.' My gut said the problem wasn't on our end, but with this, we couldn't be too sure.

'What do we do,' asked Chikondi, 'if we hear nothing?'

'What we came here to do,' Elena said. 'We've received no mission updates, so that means the mission stands. We do our job here, we go to Votum, we do our job there, we go home, and we find out what happened.'

I stared at her, and the weight of what she was saying sunk in. From my internal sense of time, we hadn't heard from OCA in seven months, which, to me, was a problem I'd discovered the day before. But of course, that wasn't the shape of things at all, not when you factored in the transit time. We hadn't heard from OCA in five and a half years. Chikondi wasn't asking what we would do *now*, in the absence of contact. He was asking about the *complete* absence of contact. The absence of any contact at all.

I remember our introductory mission briefing about Opera at OCA Oceania. Sophie Thomas, one of my favourite people on the planetary science team, led the presentation that day with her usual energetic charm.

'This one's going to be a real kick in the tits,' she said cheerily. 'The surface of this planet is almost entirely ocean.'

'Water ocean?' Elena asked, taking notes on her tablet.

'Yes,' Sophie said. 'So you don't need to worry if your boots get wet, but you haven't exactly got a fine choice of landing sites, either.' A map appeared on the screen behind her. 'There are four small islands, and your survey activity will be limited to those locations, plus however far out you can fly your drones in a given day.'

'Four islands,' Chikondi repeated. 'On the whole planet.'

'That's right.'

'When you say *small*,' Jack said, 'd'you mean, like, there's room for a quaint fishing village but you won't have many dining options, or glorified rocks?'

'Glorified rocks,' Sophie said. 'You'll be able to go for a short walk, and that's about it.'

Elena twirled her stylus as she processed that. 'That *is* a kick in the tits.'

In the control room, looking at the satmaps of the planet below us, our demeanour was far less flippant. No one was smiling. I doubt even Sophie Thomas would have smiled in the face of the two big problems conveyed by our satellites.

Problem the first: they'd only found three islands. The one we were supposed to land on first was missing.

'Could the folks back home have made a mistake?' I asked. I doubted it, but as a scientist, you have to consider every possibility.

'No,' Jack said. 'I reviewed the landing maps with them.'

'We all did,' Elena said. 'There should be something right *there*.' She pointed at the screen.

'Those maps were made over forty years ago,' I said. 'Something must have happened. Some kind of volcanic event, maybe?'

'Maybe,' Jack said, 'or an impact event. That could do it.'

'Could be sea level rise,' Elena said. 'The planet could be undergoing some kind of climate change.'

'That'd be consistent with an impact event,' Jack said.

'Or any number of things.' She gestured emptily at the map. 'We don't have any data. There's no visible crater. There's just . . . water.'

'All right,' I said, 'we'll solve this mystery later. We can sic the cubesats on it. For now . . . foul weather protocol?' Foul weather protocol is a fancy way of saying that the landing schedule OCA provides us with is a guideline, not a mandate. They know their info will be outdated by the time we arrive, and as with all things, we have autonomy over making changes as needed. If a landing site doesn't work out for any reason, we have the freedom to mix things up.

'About that,' Jack said. He rotated the satmap on screen so that we could see the other three islands. Except we *couldn't* see them, because of the second problem: the grand majority of Opera was choked with raging storm clouds. We could see flashes of lightning, grey swirls of hurricane. The textbook example of what *foul weather protocol* was intended for. We'd seen storm clouds out the window, naturally, but we hadn't realised the global scale we were dealing with.

Elena was fixated on the cloud patterns, her expression conflicted. The meteorologist in her was fascinated. The astronaut who needed to put a spacecraft down was concerned.

'What if I put us into a stationary orbit for a few days?' I said. 'We can collect more satellite data, we can see if the storms ease up, and we can make an informed decision from there.'

'Agreed,' Elena said.

Jack was antsy to land, but he nodded. 'Yeah, that's smart.'

I turned my head. 'Chikondi? Consensus?'

Chikondi blinked himself back from wherever he'd been. 'Sure,' he said. 'That's fine.'

*

For ten days, we waited and watched.

The storms did not ease up.

Our island did not reappear.

Our comms folders remained empty.

'We're wasting time,' Jack said. 'We're not learning anything more than a probe would.'

'Those storm systems are going to last weeks,' Elena said, standing on solid data at last. 'And those wind speeds—'

'Are something we know now. We can do the math.'

'This isn't landing a fucking rover packed in airbags. We're talking human bodies.'

'Yeah, *my* human body, I'm aware. It's not doing anybody any good just dicking around up here.'

'It's not going to do anybody any good smashed to shit down there, either.'

'Will you both please stop?' I said wearily.

Jack folded his hands around the back of his head and exhaled, looking at the satmap. His face shifted.

'What?' I asked.

'What about the shallows?' he said. He pointed at a region in the planet's northern hemisphere. 'This whole stretch right here. Radar says the water there's – what? Between one to two meters deep?'

Elena squinted. 'You want to land in the water.'

'I'm saying we *could* land on the *rock* that's *under* a small amount of water. Look. The weather's not as bad there.'

'It's still bad.'

'But not *as* bad. You can land in those wind speeds. And the worst of it's way up here, yeah?' He circled his hand over the angry swirls on the map. 'That'd put us out of harm's way.'

'No,' Elena said, speaking to the idea in general. 'We could land the main craft in shallow water, we could anchor it to the rock, but we can't inflate the modules. They haven't got solid floors, nothing would stay in place.'

'We can set up some of the lab equipment up here. We just won't bring samples inside.'

'I'm not thinking about the lab, I'm thinking about the greenhouse.'

'True,' Jack said, 'but I'm not saying we stay in the shallows long term. Just until one of our other sites opens up. You said the storm systems could last weeks. So, we go a few weeks without eating our vegetables. Sounds like my childhood.'

'And your adulthood,' I added.

He shot me a quick wink. 'We'll live.'

'What about the airlocks?' Elena said.

'What about them?' he said.

'Two meters at high tide, estimated. That means we can't go outside during that time.'

'We can schedule around it. Fieldwork during low tide, lab work during high tide.'

'*Partial* lab work. You won't have a full lab.'

Jack groaned with frustration. 'Fuck me, can you *please* try to focus on the possible here? We're allowed to be flexible with protocol when the situation demands.' He gestured at the satmap with both hands. 'This is a *bad* situation. I'm trying to work with it. Our other option is to orbit indefinitely, which would continue to be a waste of time. Or we can just leave and go on to Votum, which would be a *colossal* waste of time.'

Elena let out a long sigh and looked at me. 'What about propulsion?' she asked.

I thought about it, carefully. 'It should be fine,' I said. 'The engines are designed to get wet.'

'They're designed for rain and snow,' she said, 'not sitting in a tidepool for a few weeks.'

'I'm aware. And granted, it wasn't tested for that . . . but it should be fine. I really think so. We can seal the engine bells as soon as they cool off.'

Elena looked at the map for a long time. I could see her

mentally going through the Herculean task of changing a plan. 'We need four for consensus,' she said. I had a feeling that was as close to *yes* as she would say aloud.

'Is he still taking a nap?' Jack said.

'I think so,' I said. I pushed off from the wall, angling myself toward the cabin deck. 'I'll go get him.'

We landed at night. We could see nothing out the windows, but the sounds from outside told me much. I heard the wind whipping around the inconvenient obstruction of our hull. I heard the lapping of the disturbed shallows. I heard rain drumming like impatient fingers. It was not a cosy storm, a curl-up-with-a-book-and-a-blanket storm. This was weather that resented us.

Heading out into an unseen landscape, even with headlamps and flashlights, is a foolish idea, so we spent the dark hours assembling a ramshackle lab. The end result was cluttered and vaguely irritating, but it was only for a few weeks, we said. We could deal with disarray for a few weeks.

I dozed off in my cabin for an hour or two before dawn. The morning light wasn't what woke me. It was a sound. A shuffling sound. A sucking sound.

I sat up and looked out. There was an animal affixed to the outside of the porthole, roughly the size (and to a lesser extent, the shape) of a rugby ball, its sandpaper skin a limp lint grey. My first thought was *slug*, but that wasn't right, because its belly was not a foot, and that's not what it was holding on with. Its point of suction was its mouth, an ovular orifice surrounded by a shaggy fringe of feelers. I could see sharp structures waiting within. It had limbs as well – twelve feeble-looking legs. The animal did not appear to use its legs for bodily support, but rather to scoot its anchoring mouth forward.

I was attempting a better look at the legs when the animal raised its stump of a tail. Two neat rows of holes opened up along its sides, and from these a bone-chilling sound rang out. I am sure to its own ears – or whatever sound receptors it had – the sound was as normal as anything. To me, it was somewhere between squealing metal and a dying horse. I was taught to be objective, as a scientist, but I cannot help the fact that I am also an animal with instincts of my own. Everything about the sound told me to run.

The sound wasn't meant for me. It wasn't a threat; it was a summons. Two more not-slugs shoved their slimy mouths into view, invited by the call of the first.

My legs were still shaky from a week and a half spent in microgravity, but I ran across the corridor anyway, entering Chikondi's cabin without a knock.

'There's a—' I began, but didn't need to explain, because Chikondi was observing a sight very much like mine on his own window. He was watching the creatures intently, taking notes on the tablet in his lap. I sat beside him on his cot, and we watched the weird little thing push itself across the thick window-pane, leaving a trail of gummy saliva in its wake. Chikondi and I watched a new species together in companionable quiet, like we'd done many times before. For a moment, I thought that everything would be okay.

The animals were not limited to our cabin windows. We could hear more of them noisily creeping across the hull, and within an hour, every window on the *Merian* had at least one of the creatures slinking across to shriek awful hellos. Within two hours, you could barely see the world beyond them.

We dubbed them *Fortisostium horribilis* in our official report, but Jack called them rats.

'Why rats?' I asked.

'Because I hate rats.' He glared at the airlock window, nearly solid grey. There was no way we could get outside with so many creatures covering the hatch, not without potentially jamming the door mechanism with their bodies and giving others opportunity to come inside. One or two, we could shoo away. This many, we'd only be asking for trouble.

'They're just checking us out,' Chikondi said. 'They're allowed to observe us, too. We're the ones in their home.'

But the rats didn't care much about us at all. It's difficult to know what their senses were, because they didn't have obvious sight organs, but our movements inside the ship were of no concern to them. We were scenery, nothing more.

Elena frowned. 'They could damage the hull if they keep this up.'

'The hull's tough,' I said. 'Plus, they're not chewing it. It's probably fine.'

She looked at me. '"Probably" has a lot of room for error.'

'Ah, get out of here,' Jack said to the rats. He'd gone into the airlock and up to the outer door. He watched the rats for a moment, annoyed at their presence. He raised a fist and pounded the door three times in quick succession. The rats were startled by him, some scattering away, others freezing in place. Jack was encouraged. 'Yeah, go on, get out of here.' He pounded the door again. This resulted in more scattering, but less than before. To Jack's consternation, other rats moved in to fill the gaps, undeterred by the angry man telling them to fuck off.

'We'll have to wait,' Chikondi said. He sat on the floor and began to sketch on his tablet. The activity did not animate him, as it typically did. He did his job, but it appeared more like muscle memory than true enthusiasm.

'I'm going to go look at the storm data again,' Elena said to me. 'Could you check on the comms?'

'I already did,' I said.

'Oh,' she said. She thought for a moment, visibly rifling through some list in her head. 'What about life support?'

'I was going to do that later, but I can do it now, if you'd prefer.'

'If you wouldn't mind,' she said, though she offered no explanation as to why. It shouldn't have mattered to Elena whether my checks were done now or three hours down the road, but clearly, it was bothering her. If I could help relieve that little bit of worry, at least, then I'd easily change my schedule. One of us needed a break that day.

I left for the upper decks, leaving Chikondi drawing by rote and Jack banging on the door.

The rats did not leave at night, nor at dawn, nor the day after. The hull was blanketed with their bodies and their spit, the combination effectively blocking out the sun. We managed to steal some looks outside, if the rats shuffled in such a way that, by chance, they left a gap in a window and one of us was there to see it. The shallows were largely featureless, but there were rocks out there – craggy pillars jutting up from the seabed like stalagmites. Jack and I took to wearing binoculars around our necks in hopes of an opening, and we eventually were able to see that the rocks were likewise covered with dense coatings of rats. In basic shape, our conical spacecraft must have seemed familiar to them: a tall thing you can crawl up and cling onto.

'Could be mating behaviour,' Jack posited.

'Could be,' Chikondi said.

'Or some other kind of seasonal thing,' I added. 'External thermometers say it's chilly out there, they might do this to get out of the water.'

Chikondi watched a pair jostle each other for space, their mouths still holding firmly to the glass. 'Or could be this is a normal day,' he said. 'Maybe they just do this, and we'll never know why.'

After two more days of staring at scaly bellies, we began to debate whether we should simply take off and find a new landing site. But we'd kill the rats in lift-off, we knew, and nobody wanted to do that, despite the obvious problem they'd become. Given the numbers we were seeing outside, though, lasting damage to their population seemed unlikely.

Opera made the decision for us. The storm system that had

been so safely distant made a sudden swing south, and the winds kicked up to a speed downright dangerous for launch. The shallows swelled and roiled. Rain lashed at our windows like a hail of arrows fired sideways. We could go nowhere.

The rats hung on to us, their port in the storm. They weren't leaving, either.

When I was a child, I was afraid of the dark. I was convinced of wicked eyes watching me from the corners, shivering hands reaching up to pull me into the void below my bed. *That's just in your imagination*, my mother told me. *Tell your imagination to go somewhere nice instead.* So when the lights went out and the door closed, and all I could hear was my own frightened breaths, I would ask myself: *Where do you want to go?* The answer went through phases, depending on age and fancy. Sometimes it was a treehouse in a peaceful meadow, the contents of which grew more and more elaborate with every night that I fussed with its interior. Sometimes it was a pirate ship, with me as the kick-ass captain, waving at the merfolk who led me to treasure. Sometimes I'd build from someone else's scaffold, replaying the best bits of a story I'd read or a game I'd played, revamping the scenes I thought could be better. The question worked, is the point, and for years, that is how I fell asleep, curled up in a nest of my mind's weavings.

I could not sleep in Opera's shallows. If it had been the storm alone, I could've acclimated to that. The wind howled like an engine, but that din was constant, certain. The rats, on the other hand . . . God, the rats. I couldn't tune them out, no matter how I tried. The human brain is conditioned to shout *danger* at unseen animal sounds, opening a fire hose of adrenaline so as to awaken you to whatever prehistoric unpleasantness is about to bite your toes or foul your grain stores or drag your babies off into the night. It didn't matter that the rats were on the other side of a wall. It didn't matter that they were only *adjacent*, not in my actual space. Their sounds were unpredictable, and my brain reacted accordingly. Pushing my blankets around my ears helped with the uneven percussion of their feet, but nothing would drown out their shrieks, which they would unleash every hour, or half hour, or a few minutes after the last, wrenching me out of whatever half-formed dream I'd managed to sink into and back into puffy-eyed misery.

With intent, I began to ask myself the question that had guided me into the deep slumbers of my childhood: *Where do you want to go?*

Mirabilis, I replied. *I want to go back to Mirabilis.*

I forcibly conjured memories of that lush world, but they had become bittersweet. I knew that those smiles would fade, those adventures would end. All days on Mirabilis led to Opera. To look at them was to look back on the path that had led to howling and skittering and sleepless nights. The ache to return to a time long gone was almost worse than fear.

If the sounds of the rats were chaos, the sounds of Elena were clockwork. I didn't need to be on the same deck as her to know what she was doing.

She left her cabin around 06:00 every morning.

She'd run a full systems diagnostic.

She'd check the comms folders, even though no notifications had been received.

She'd check on the airlocks to see if the rats had given us an opening.

She'd go over that day's weather data from the cubesats. She'd study it with meticulous focus, then update her forecasts accordingly.

She'd exercise for an hour. Weights, rowing machine, treadmill.

She'd shower, ten minutes.

She'd work on a project. Sometimes it was reviewing her old

reports, rewriting sections she'd had better thoughts about, then rewriting them again. Sometimes she'd go through the cargo hold, rechecking the inventory. Sometimes I had no idea what she was working on, because she didn't want to explain.

I awoke one morning to her knock on my cabin door. Jack's knock is a melody, if he knocks at all, and he never waits for a response. Chikondi's is a polite drumming, almost a little too quiet. Elena's knock is three solid taps, loud and direct. I glanced at my clock after I heard it. 05:36. I'd managed about forty-three minutes of sleep from the last time I checked it. I sat up and rubbed my face. 'Yeah,' I called.

'Hey,' she said as she entered. There was a softness to her voice that I hadn't heard in a while, and I warmed to it. 'Sorry to wake you.'

'It's okay,' I said. 'What's up?'

'It can wait,' she said.

'I'm awake now.'

She stuck her hands in her pockets and leaned against the door frame. 'I was thinking about doing a hardware inspection.'

'Okay,' I said. 'Of which system?'

'All of them,' she said.

I blinked. 'All of them.'

'I know, it's a lot of work.' An understatement. A full, proper, by-the-book hardware inspection took days. 'But we've been sitting in water for three weeks, and those things—' As if on cue, a chorus of shrieking erupted. We covered our ears and waited for it to end. 'Those things outside are doing God knows what out there.'

None of that would impact the internal hardware, but I knew she knew that. 'We've got green lights across the board,' I said. 'Have you noticed any malfunctions? Anything acting up?'

'No. I just—' She looked restless, on edge. 'I just think it doesn't hurt to check. Better safe than sorry.'

I rubbed my face again. My temples throbbed. My eyes

twinged. I felt drunk, and not in the fun way. Flimsy thoughts strained for one another, evaporating before connection could be made. 'Okay,' I said. 'Sure, we can do that.' We stared at each other for a moment. 'Did you mean right now?'

She put up her palms. 'Whenever you're up for it. I know it's a pain,' she said. Her face gave a different answer. *Yes*, it said. *Right now*.

I got dressed, and we got to work.

'Okay, let's give it a go,' Jack said.

I lay in the cockpit, my control panel lit and ready. At Jack's suggestion, I'd reworked the launch sequence to allow us to simply 'rev up' the engines without heading into full lift-off. They'd rumble a bit, enough to be loud, and without causing thrust. A rumble is all we were after. We were hoping to scare the rats off. The wind still prevented us from launch, but in lieu of that, we might be able to go outside. And if *that* wasn't safe, then at least we would be rat-free, even if only temporarily. Uninterrupted sleep sounded like victory enough.

I got on the comms. 'Engine test commencing,' I said.

I hit the right buttons. Outside, the engines rumbled good and proper. Some Pavlovian part of me reflexively reacted to the sound with excitement; I reminded it we were going nowhere.

A second sound emerged. A split second after the engines kicked in, every rat on the hull began shrieking in alarm.

'Jesus *Christ*,' Jack said, slamming his hands over his ears.

The din made me shut my eyes, but I forced them open to look at the window. The rats, by their standards, were bellowing, the vocal holes in their sides straining as wide as they could. But I noticed something else, something that made my stomach sink. The viscosity of their mouths changed. They were clinging on tighter. In the face of danger, they held fast.

'Give it another minute,' Jack yelled.

'It's not working,' I shouted back.

'Just another minute.'

We sat in the noise for a few seconds more, the hellish harmony of straining metal and terrified animals clawing its way into my teeth, my torso. I looked at my readouts. I looked at the stubborn fuckers clinging to the window. I turned the engines off.

The rats took several minutes more to calm down.

'Shit,' Jack said, wiping his brow as they quieted.

I let my eyes fall shut, savouring the relative peace. The storm still bellowed, but that much I could manage. 'It makes sense, with what we know of them,' I said. 'If they evolved alongside storms like this, and if their response to them is to find a rock and hang on, then maybe . . . maybe they interpret noise and rumbling as the weather getting worse.'

'They double-down, is what you're saying.'

'Maybe.'

Jack shook his head. 'It was a stupid idea,' he said. 'I shouldn't have suggested it.'

'It wasn't,' I said. 'We had to do it to know that it wouldn't work.'

He shook his head again. 'Stupid,' he repeated. He climbed down the ladder without another word.

Chikondi's cabin door was closed, so I knocked.

'Come in,' he said. He was sitting cross-legged on the bed as I entered, watching the rats on the window. His tablet lay on the floor nearby, switched off.

'Why are your lights out?' I asked. It was mid-afternoon.

'I was trying to get a feel for the sunlight,' he said. 'Such as it is, anyway.' There wasn't much of that to see. You could see a little, shining weakly through the rainwater that ran without pause through the gaps between silhouettes. The effect was like stained glass in reverse, in a grim sort of way.

I sat on the bed beside him, likewise pulling myself cross-legged.

We sat in silence, watching the rats shuffle. I glanced at him, remembering when he'd been a baby-faced trainee with a million ideas. I wondered what that kid would think of the lean, serious man, pondering fragments in the dark. I wondered what he'd think of me.

I reached out and rubbed my knuckle over his cheek. 'You could use a shave,' I said.

He gave a single chuckle. 'I probably could.'

We sat quietly, again. 'Out with it,' I said. 'Whatever it is.'

Chikondi exhaled. 'Do you think it's right for us to be here?'

'Elaborate.'

He nodded at the rats. 'We're annoyed with them because they're in our way. But they're in their element. This is their niche, not ours.'

'Species migrate,' I said. 'Most of evolutionary history can be summed up as chance encounters between species that hadn't crossed paths before.'

'We're not migrating, we're sticking our noses in. We're not here because we need food or territory. We're here because we want to be. We're flipping over rocks because we're curious.'

'You've always been a guy who likes flipping over rocks.'

'Yes, *I* like it. The animals underneath do not. Say there are worms under the rock. Worms hate sunlight. It hurts them. Is it fair to the worms, to cause them pain so that I can know more about them?'

'You always put the rock back. *We* always put the rocks back.'

'It still hurts before we do so. Is that a fair trade, their pain for our knowledge?'

'If that knowledge means we can do right by the general population of these figurative worms? That we can alter our behaviours and practices so that everything in an ecosystem, worms included, won't be harmed in the future? Yes, I think that's a very fair trade. A sacrifice on behalf of one, or a few, to benefit the many.'

'You can only call it sacrifice if it's consensual. Nobody asked the worms under the rock what they thought about the whole thing.'

'If we don't hurt a few worms, we won't know that worms *can* be hurt. That path's got far more potential for destruction.'

'You think so?'

'You don't?'

He thought silently. 'I probably do,' he said at last. 'But I don't know right now.'

I watched him as he watched the rats. 'What are you looking forward to most about going home?'

He blinked. 'What?'

'Where's the first place you're going to go, once we're out of quarantine?'

I'd thrown him off of his mental track, and I could see him struggling to shift gears. 'A cafe,' he said.

'Huh,' I said. 'Any particular cafe?'

'No,' he said. 'I don't care which.' He looked at me; I was still waiting. 'The sort that looks like they cleaned out their grandmother's garage and put everything they found on the walls. Comfortable chairs. Good music, but not too loud. I want a cold drink and a dessert that looks ridiculous, and I want to sit in a corner and read a book and listen to conversations I don't understand between people I don't know.'

I instantly understood the appeal of his last point, and did not take offense. 'What kind of book?'

'I . . . I don't know.'

'Sure you do. Come on.'

He considered. A little smile pushed at his cheeks. 'Something with a heist.'

I laughed. 'Since when do you read heists?'

He shrugged. 'I don't. Just seems like the sort of thing you read at a cafe while eating dessert.'

'Okay,' I said. 'And where is this cafe? Back in Lusaka, or near campus, or someplace you've never been?'

'I really don't care,' he said. 'Cafes are pretty much the same wherever you go.'

'I'd—'

My answer was cut short by the scream of a rat. Chikondi and I jumped. The sound died down within a few seconds, but Chikondi remained shaken. I looked down at the sheet and saw it gripped between his fingers, as if he might fall. I'd gotten five cumulative hours of sleep the night before; how had he fared?

I took his clenched hand within mine. He relaxed, just a touch.

Where do you want to go?

Home, I thought. But where was that, now? The *Merian* had fit that bill for years, but she no longer felt like home, just a machine we were trapped inside. Did I want my parents' apartment, the one I'd grown up in? Someone else owned it now, surely, if it hadn't been torn down. The latter was the more likely scenario, I figured. I imagined the walls of my childhood room, such a sturdy, immutable fortress then. I imagined them being torn apart by construction equipment, cheerful paint giving way to raw wood and bent nails and weary insulation, a space within a space, an impermanent dimension in the place that had been an eternal refuge.

A new home, then. I forced myself to entertain the thought, despite the headache I could not shake, a product of both the steady noise and my growing malnutrition. What kind of home did I want? A city apartment? A rural house? Did I want a place of my own, a place to set roots and settle, or would I be content to rent furnished rooms, bouncing from country to country as whim or opportunity suggested?

The rats shrieked. Thunder growled. Choppy waves smacked the hull. I gave up on the questions. I couldn't cosy up in the future. The present was far too loud.

Please let me sleep, I thought. It was a wretched plea,

transmitted in no direction in particular but asked from the bottom of my heart all the same. *Please, please let me sleep.*

I did not.

Elena ducked her head out of the guts of the water filtration system, a wrench in her gloved hand. 'Do you think they could come through the hull?' she asked.

I blinked, lowering my flashlight. 'The hull that can withstand micrometeoroids at half the speed of light.'

'A single impact is different than something scratching all day, every day. Could they erode the outer plating?'

'No,' I said, but now I didn't know. Could they? The notion seemed ridiculous.

. . . but *could they*?

'They won't get inside,' I reassured her, despite my lack of certainty. 'I'm sure of it.'

'Okay, that's good,' Elena said. She paused in thought. 'Even if they don't get in, could they damage the hull in such a way that might compromise our safety in flight?'

I stared at her. I hadn't considered this. 'I doubt it.'

'But is it *possible*?'

'I—' My mind itched now, wondering what other dangerous possibilities I hadn't thought to examine. 'I'll have to think about it.'

She nodded, glad that I was taking her question seriously. She continued to inspect every pipe, every wire. We'd done a full inspection like this four times in the past two months. A strange part of me *wanted* to find something wrong, something that would tell Elena her gut feeling had been right, something was amiss, but hey, our diligence paid off. We solved a problem before it happened. We prevented catastrophe.

Instead, we found nothing. Again.

The more nothing we found, the less she trusted it.

*

I had no reason to join Jack in the data lab, and would have kept walking, were it not for one muttered word:

'Idiot.'

I stepped back and ducked my head in the door. 'Who is?'

He hadn't realised I was there, his expression said. He shook his head and gestured at the monitor. 'Cubesats finished mapping the sea floor.'

'And?' I walked into the room and glanced over the screen. Opera's surface was spread out before us, flattened like a fur pelt. Water-filled canyons were carved deep into the rock, teasing us with secrets our hydrodrones could reveal if only there were a way to launch them. 'Isn't a map good?'

'There's no evidence of a recent impact event.'

I wasn't sure what he was getting at. A dim memory surfaced: him suggesting that possibility upon arrival. 'Well, we can rule that out, then.'

'It was a stupid thing to suggest,' he said.

'No, it wasn't.'

'We had no data. I was talking out of my arse, like always.'

I frowned at him. 'It was just an idea. We toss around wrong ideas all the time.'

He wasn't listening to me. He shook his head at the sea floor maps. 'This is my fault.'

'What is?'

'Landing in the shallows was my idea. It's my fault we're stuck here.'

I stared hard at him. I wasn't entertaining this. 'We had consensus. We all agreed.'

'I don't know why,' he snapped. 'You should know by now that I never know what the fuck I'm talking about. I'm just bullshit with a big smile. I always knew it was going to catch up with me, and now it has, and it's fucked all of you over as well.'

'Jack—'

He stood up, and stormed out. A banging rang through the ship a few minutes later. He was trying to scare the rats off the windows again.

Chikondi's cabin door was closed, so I knocked. He didn't answer. I went in anyway.

He lay in bed, partially clothed, hands folded on his chest. He didn't welcome me, but he didn't turn me away, either. I sat on the end of his bed.

'Is there some kind of event you'd like to see when we're back home?' I asked. 'Some kind of festival, or holiday, or—?'

He shut his eyes. 'I don't know.'

'So think about it.'

He sighed. 'The World Cup,' he said. 'If the World Cup still exists, I want to go see the World Cup, wherever it is.'

I nodded with approval. 'I'd like to see a solar eclipse.'

He craned his head up from the pillow. 'You've never seen a solar eclipse?'

'Partial, sure. I want to see totality.'

'You're an astronaut. Wouldn't an eclipse rank low for you, given all you've seen?'

'I don't know. I've never seen one. Have you?'

'Yes.'

'Where?'

'Home,' he said. '2095. I think it was June. My parents took the day off work so we could take a car out and see it together.' There was a smile at first, but then a faltering, a sombre remembrance that pulled him toward the past, not the future. The opposite direction I wanted to steer him in.

'Tell me about the World Cup,' I said. 'Pretending that all the same countries are still around, who would you want—'

He gently stopped me with a raised hand. 'Ariadne, I – I see what you're trying to do. I appreciate it, I do. But I'd really like to be alone right now. I'm sorry.'

I swallowed. I nodded. 'Come find me if you change your mind,' I said with a forced smile. I squeezed his leg, and I left.

In the first two months, I would go to bed at night and cross my fingers that the storm would be gone in the morning.

In the third month, I begged whoever might be listening to stop the storm, to let us go.

In the fourth month, I began to forget that life could be any different.

I walked past Elena, going through her inspection checklist step by step. It didn't matter that I wouldn't help her anymore. She still needed to check.

I walked past Jack, kicking the airlock door. 'Stupid,' he said. 'You're so fucking stupid.' The rats paid him no mind.

I went to the cabin deck. Chikondi's door was closed, so I knocked. He didn't answer. I put my ear up to the door. I could hear his movement within the room. I did not go inside, not when I was not wanted.

I went to my cabin and lay down in bed, the blanket up to my chin.

Where do you want to go?

I tried to visit my imagined childhood treehouse, but there were rats – real rats – running in the corners and flies crawling on the ceiling and black mould eating away the wood.

I tried to board my pirate ship, but the merfolk pulled their cold lips back and laughed through ragged teeth. They only wanted to see me drown.

I tried to remember stories I'd drawn strength from, but I could only remember the skeleton shape of them, not the beating heart within. Their warmth had gone cold.

Where do you want to go?

I couldn't answer that. There was nowhere *to* go. There was nowhere but this. There would never be anything but this.

*

The next day, I got up. I didn't want to, but I did. I don't know why. There was no good reason to.

I went down to the control room. Elena was in there, running her morning systems diagnostic. We didn't say anything to each other. There was nothing *to* say.

A flash on the comms monitor caught my eye. A tiny spark of hope shot through me, but it died quickly. The notification wasn't anything from OCA. Just the morning's weather data, freshly downloaded from the cubesats.

I glanced at Elena. Her diagnostics looked to be half complete. I knew she'd sit vigil until they were done. I also knew that she'd look at the weather data in turn, so there was no rush for me to open it. I did anyway. It was something to do.

I have learned, in the years I've spent working by Elena's side, what all the swirls and colours mean on a weather chart. I lack her honed sense for an atmosphere's choreography, but I can read the map. There was one particular change that morning that caught my eye.

'Elena,' I said.

'Mmm?'

'Can you come look at this?'

She glanced at my screen. 'I'll do the weather map when I'm done here.' Everything in its precious order.

I stood up, swivelled her chair toward my monitor, and pointed. 'Tell me this is what I think it is.'

Her eyes narrowed at my disruption, then widened at my suggestion. She rushed over. 'How did I miss this?'

'Weather does unpredictable things,' I said.

She'd taught me that ever-present rule, but it wasn't explanation enough for her. She'd spent every day on Opera in a desperate defence *against* the unpredictable. Anything that happened, she wanted – *needed* to have a game plan waiting for it.

The thing was, she'd spent so much time focused on what

could go wrong, she'd forgotten the possibility of something going right.

'I'll get the boys,' I said, hurrying toward the ladder.

Chikondi's door was closed. I did not knock. I stuck my head right inside.

'Control room,' I said. He sat up in bed to look at me. 'You want to see this.' I didn't wait for his reply, nor did I shut the door.

I found Jack sitting slumped in the cargo hold, glaring emptily at the airlock. I took his hand and led him upstairs.

Elena still looked bothered to be in a reality she hadn't anticipated. 'There's . . . there's a drop in wind speed.' Her eyes darted around the map, still expecting a mistake. 'Doesn't look like it'll last long. Maybe a day or two, given these pressure systems.'

Chikondi sat up a little straighter.

'How much of a drop?' Jack asked.

She looked him in the eye. 'Enough.'

I saw a spark in him that had been lost for months. 'What about the other landing sites?'

She reoriented the map, bringing each island into focus. None of their prognoses were good. Four months, and still, the only ground on Opera was inaccessible.

'We could orbit for a while,' Jack said hesitantly. 'Global storms that last this long – I mean, we've seen that on gas giants—'

'Dust storms on Mars,' I added.

'—but not rain. This is new. We could . . . we could make something of our time here.' He sounded unconvinced of his own words, as if they were what he knew he should say but nothing more.

Elena thought. 'It'd be a waste of that time,' she said. 'There's nothing we could do from orbit that a team of researchers back home couldn't do with the same data. You don't send bodies if all you're going to do is study satmaps. That's not what we're here for. That's not what we were sent to do.'

The room was silent for a while. Nobody needed to say what we all knew: none of us wanted to stay. We wanted to be gone, as far from this place as the universe would allow. We had spent a third of a year on Opera, and we came back with a one-sided portrait of a single new species and an inconclusive parcel of weather data. We had gained nothing.

'We could leave a couple of cubesats in orbit,' I said, 'so that people back home *can* study this.'

'That works,' Elena said. 'There'll be plenty to dig into.'

We were quiet again. 'Consensus?' Jack said.

'Yes,' I said.

'Yes,' Elena said.

Chikondi nodded.

Nobody moved for a moment. Were we abandoning our mission? Or were we doing what we needed – what *we,* as living animals, needed – for that mission to continue?

I still haven't made up my mind about that.

Jack broke the silence. 'Let's start prep.' There was no discussion about it. Consensus had been unnecessary; we'd given it months before.

Everybody got right to it, putting away the lab equipment that had never been used, packing up the tools left here and there. I admit that we were not careful. We didn't do things perfectly. We didn't use our checklists. We just threw things in boxes, tied them down, and moved on to the next. A door had been opened, and we'd be damned if we let it close.

Launching a spacecraft is a violent act. For all our fine technology, all the wondrous advancements we love to pat ourselves on the back about, the process of leaving a planet has always been the same: push as hard and fly as fast as possible. I had been through over a dozen launches before Opera. I was always overwhelmed by the experience, awed by the raw power at my back – and yes, obviously, a little bit afraid. I've heard some astronauts describe the feeling as like somebody putting a massive foot in the middle of your back and pushing you away. I never imagined a foot. I imagined the hands of every scientist and supporter, lifting us up to a place no one could reach alone.

Leaving Opera felt different.

It *wasn't* different, I know this – not in mechanics, not in process, not in anything but context. We were strapped in, systems nominal. The engines roared. The seats rattled. I did not feel supportive hands as we lifted away. I felt the reverse: the grasp of a planet that did not want us to escape. My body sagged into itself as the G-forces clocked up and up. The *Merian* erupted in a chorus of metallic squealing as it fought against Opera's impartial physics. We were no longer riding a spacecraft, but a tiny bird, caught in a vast pit of tar, beating her wings so hard she risked leaving a piece of herself behind.

The rats were terrified. Some had fallen with the initial blast, but others were still clinging to the goddamn windows, too stupid to understand that the longer they held fast, the more certain their doom. I watched their shuddering bodies as the rushing air sent them flailing, as the ones that did not fall were swallowed in flame and rendered ash. I felt nothing but quiet loathing toward them, and the purity of that feeling was the ugliest I've ever felt. *It's not their fault*, the good scientist in me feebly argued. *They meant no harm. This is a terrible death. They don't deserve this.*

I don't care, the raw spite in me replied. And I didn't. For all my impartiality, for all my trying to set aside anthropocentric biases and see the beauty in all forms, I truly didn't care. I watched them burn, and felt a twisted gratitude.

I have never stopped hating what that says about me.

As if someone had thrown a switch, everything changed. The last wisp of atmosphere melted away. Where clouds had menaced, stars now glittered. My limbs, my head, my chest lifted away from the chair, pushing against the straps that kept me down. I unbuckled my harness without so much as a glance at the readouts, protocol be damned. I shut my eyes. I let my body go limp. I floated in all directions and none, the concept of weight forgotten. I bit my lip hard to stifle the whimper that bubbled up in my throat. It was the moment when the painkillers kick in, the sip of water that keeps you from dying.

More. I needed more.

I flipped myself around, headed straight for the cargo hold, and got myself into my EVA suit. I could hear the others calling me, but their words didn't stick.

'Hey,' Jack said. He put his hand on the window of the airlock as I prepared to let myself outside. 'What are you doing?'

'I need to check for damage,' I said. This was true. We hadn't been able to inspect the outer hull, and though we'd clearly been okay for launch, I needed to make sure the rats hadn't damaged anything vital.

Jack opened his mouth to argue with me. Elena appeared behind him, and put her hand on his shoulder. 'She's right,' she said. 'Let her check.'

The airlock opened before me, edgeless vacuity beyond. There were no winds here, no crashing waves. Only the cold constancy of stars, to which I was just a crude bit of wet carbon, a flake of skin you brush aside. My pain and pettiness and mistakes and inadequacies did not matter. I did not matter. Nothing we did out here mattered. Nothing we could or would ever do would matter, in the face of this.

My comms crackled on. 'Ari, your tether,' Jack said. 'You forgot your tether.'

I hadn't forgotten. I just hadn't brought it.

I tested the metal handholds in the airlock below my thick gloves, like a kid getting ready to let go of the side of the pool and kick off into the deep end. I didn't know what I was doing.

I hadn't thought any of this through. All I knew was that one of my options was easy. So easy.

'Ari – son of a bitch—'

Elena took over the comms, her voice cool and hard. 'If you're going to inspect damage, that's fine, but you have to follow protocol. If you can't do it now, come back in and do it later.'

I let go of one of the handholds. I raised my finger, traced it over the stars. God, they were beautiful. How had something as crude as us ever come from something so beautiful?

I could hear Jack in the background. 'I'm getting my fucking suit—'

'She's got the airlock open, you can't—'

'Well, *she* can't, either! Ari, listen—'

The comms went silent again. I took a breath. That's all I could hear – my own breath. No screaming wind, no endless waves, no slimy mouths sucking. I heard nothing but the air travelling in and out of me. This was good. This was good. I didn't want anything but this, not ever. I didn't even need to look at the stars anymore. Just knowing they were there and that there was no wall between us was enough. I could live behind my own eyelids. This was good.

I heard the comms switch back on. For a moment, all that greeted me was silence.

'Ariadne,' Chikondi said.

I opened my eyes.

'Ariadne, come back inside.'

I turned toward the airlock door, away from the calming dark and back toward the harsh lights and oppressive walls. Only, it didn't look as bad as before. It didn't look as bad because Chikondi was there, floating on the other side of the window, his palm pressed toward me.

'Do you want a pet,' he asked, 'when we go home?'

I stared at him.

'I'd like to get a dog,' he said. 'I've never had a dog before. My brothers were allergic, but I'm not.'

I shut my eyes. I didn't want a dog. I wanted the stars. I wanted no walls.

'I think I'd like a beagle. Not too big, not too small. I like their ears. Davide in astrophysics had a beagle, do you remember him?'

My breath caught, then quickened. I wanted him to go away, I wanted all of them to disappear. *I* wanted to disappear.

'Come on, Ari. We need you in here.' He pressed his hand harder against the window. 'In *here*.'

'I—' I hadn't cared what I was doing when I'd gone out there, but now the lack of that knowledge confused me. What was I doing? Who was I right then?

'I know,' he said, even though I'd said nothing else. He gave me a sad smile. 'I know. Come on.'

I let the door close, the pressure equalise. Jack pulled me inside. Elena removed my helmet, my gloves. Chikondi pulled me out of the cocoon of my suit. I could still hear my own breath, but it was quieter, and I could hear theirs, too, every breath and heartbeat as they held me close – as we all held each other, floating in the centre of the room, no beginning or end to us.

Votum

Our species evolved for a world that spins. The lengthy days and nights of our planet's poles prove challenging for our diurnal minds, inviting summer insomnia and winter depression. Falling and staying asleep was one of the most common frustrations for early 21st-century astronauts living aboard the International Space Station, who saw the sun come up every hour and a half in their constant gravitational free-fall. But steady planetary rotation is not a given in the universe, nor even the norm. Red dwarf systems have a tendency toward tidal locking – a state in which an object's rotational period is the same length of time as its orbital period. To illustrate this more simply: think about the way our Moon looks from Earth. When looking up at a full Moon on a clear night, you will always see the same friendly arrangement of craters shining back. Some cultures see a face in the Moon; others, a rabbit. Whatever the interpretation, the underlying truth remains the same. One side of the Moon is always facing Earth. The far side never does. This is a tidal lock.

It is unusual that it took us until Votum to land on a world that holds still. Aecor is tidally locked with its parent planet, but not its star, so it experiences night and day in regular rhythm, just as Luna does (you'll know the lunar day cycle as a slow exchange of shadow and light – the phases). If Mirabilis and Opera had thin atmospheres, they likely would be locked with Zhenyi, but their thick quilts of clouds have a spin of their own, pushing against the surface as they whip around. This nudging is powerful enough to make a planet turn (an effect you can see on Venus as well).

In this regard, Votum, with its textbook tidal lock, is a more conventional planet. With an atmosphere only sixteen percent the thickness of Earth's, there is not enough force to shove the mountains forward. One side is in permanent darkness, the other in daylight. As if this were not challenging enough, Votum's close proximity to Zhenyi also means heavy bombardment by solar particles. The robust magnetic field that surrounds Votum helps, but there's only so much that can be done. The combination of these factors means the surface temperatures are extreme, and protection from Zhenyi's rays is minimal. It is not a leisurely place, this little world.

We astronauts are already protected from dangers like these in the nakedness of deep space, but travelling to a planet such as this – one that stands forever unblinking in the face of its sun – was new territory for OCA. We had not, when I left Earth, sent any crewed missions to the hot surface of Mercury, and the other Lawki missions were still in their first legs of transit when the *Merian* took off. We weren't sure what to expect, physiologically. So, to be on the safe side, my skin's appetite for radiation was increased, providing me with an extra layer of in-built sunscreen. And while our survey schedule would take us to the planet's frozen shadow, our first stop was the sunny side. Our antifreeze would not help us there, and we did not have a supplementation on hand for *losing* heat instead of retaining it. We warm-blooded mammals are a nuisance that way. This challenge is one that *does* require a technological solution – our TEVA suits, whose full spread of climate controls would be deployed at last.

That is all I awoke with on Votum: a thicker skin and the tools I already carried. I floated in front of the mirror, studying my unclothed form. There was nothing about me that appeared different than it had on Opera, not in a visual, touchable way.

But I *was* different, as different as a stranger. My mind felt quiet, at last, but the feeling was so precious that I was reluctant to accept it. I had become so accustomed to the cacophony that part of me perversely wished for it, more trusting of unending discord than peace that could be snatched away. I would never again be the Ariadne who had not been to Opera, just as I would never again be the Ariadne who had never left Earth, just as I would never again be the Ariadne who had never left her parents' home, who had never bled, who had yet to learn to walk. A moth *was* a caterpillar, once, but it no longer *is* a caterpillar. It cannot break itself back down, cannot metamorphose in reverse. To try to eat leaves again would mean starvation. Crawling back into the husk would provide no shelter. It is a paradox – the impossibility of reclaiming that which lies behind, housed within a form comprised entirely of the repurposed pieces of that same past. We exist where we begin, yet to remain there is death.

But I'm not a moth. I'm human. And in humans, there are far more stages than just two. I could not have predicted each version of me that I shifted into, but through my history, one constant has always remained true: change itself. I might not be able to return to the other Ariadnes, but I would not always be the Ariadne floating in front of the mirror, either. I did not know who she was, the one waiting for me to start moving toward her. I was curious about her, all the same. I was eager to meet her.

I cut my nails. I put on my clothes. I left my cabin to find my crew.

Elena refused the dice roll on Votum. She said she'd already been the first somewhere, and that the honour should be Chikondi's. He protested; she won in the end.

He stood for a long time at the bottom of the ramp as he took the world in. Nobody teased him, as they had when I stepped onto Aecor. We did not rush him. We would rush nothing here.

I nearly collapsed at feeling dirt beneath my feet once more. I wanted to roll in it, burrow in it, rub it onto my cheeks. There was nothing *but* dirt before us – a bouldered plain, devoid of any sign of life. Mountains marked the horizon, ambling up toward the orange sky. Zhenyi hung large but dim as ever, and the thin atmosphere allowed a modest flocking of the brightest stars through, despite the unending day.

Jack sat down and dragged his fingers through the dirt. He picked some up and examined it in his palm, brushing the grains this way and that. I don't know what he was doing, or looking for. I think he was just a man playing with dirt. I had no interest in interrupting that.

Some may have looked at Votum and seen a wasteland. This was the polar opposite of Mirabilis, the empty balance to its bounty. Aecor had been a quiet world, too, but even before we'd seen the shimmering swimmers, the waters beneath the ice held promise, and the cyclical respiration of the geysers told us the planet had a pulse. But Votum . . . nothing moved on Votum, nothing but pebbles small enough to be caught by wind.

I knew OCA had debated sending us here, but there is much to be learned from a habitable-zone planet that has either died out or on which life never got started. Knowledge from the former can be used as a cautionary tale; knowledge from the latter gets us closer to understanding why life begins in the first place. Either way, we get a few more clues toward the biggest Why of all.

I didn't care about any of the whys or hows, in that moment. I didn't see a waste, either. When I looked out at Votum, at that vast, echoing flatland, I saw exactly what my soul had longed for. A quiet place. A blank slate. A reality in which everything held still for however long I needed it to. If things moved, it would be because I moved, because I chose to move. It was not exciting, but neither was it frightening. It was not compelling, but neither was it overwhelming. It *was*, pure and simple. Neutrality incarnate.

I lay down. I pressed my palms against the ground. I affixed myself to Votum's outer curve, traversing the galaxy along with it. I had my back in the dirt, but I felt as though I were floating in saltwater. The sky saturated my eyes. Time dissolved. I continued to breathe deep. In and out. In and out. Votum did not need me, but I needed it. I had needed it desperately.

'Should we make camp?' Chikondi asked at last.

It was the obvious thing to do, the next step in protocol. Elena looked out at the horizon with a dogged gaze. 'Later,' she said. She took a step forward, testing the light gravity. She took another step, then another, and another. I propped myself up just in time to see her break into a run. Her body wasn't accustomed to Votum's pull yet, but you could see a well-honed stride beneath her stumbling, the legs that remembered how to run marathons and dance all night. Jack watched her for a moment, then took off after. The strength in each step was visible, palpable. It was like watching someone release a coiled spring.

Chikondi reached out to me. 'Come on,' he said.

I let him pull me up, and we took off together, barrelling after the other two. Elena knew where she was headed. I did not, but I trusted her. Jack had full confidence in his ability to keep up. I did not, but if he could, I could. And Chikondi – Chikondi wasn't much of an athlete, but I could see him savour the way he hung in the air for a fraction of a second after every wobbly step. He didn't care where the destination was or whether he looked good getting there. If he found joy in awkwardness, then I would, too.

We ran to the top of a small hill, panting hard as we reached the crest. The desert stretched out below us – angular, crumbling, warm red, like the place that exists below a campfire.

Elena surveyed. She put her hand on Jack's shoulder congenially; he put his hand over hers. 'It's beautiful,' she said.

Chikondi and I walked panting up beside them. I leaned my

helmet against his arm. He offered his hand to Elena. She took it gladly. We became a molecule, distinct components attached by natural bonds.

'It is beautiful,' I replied, looking out at the nothing. 'It's the most beautiful thing I've ever seen.'

The airlock hissed open and we poured ourselves inside, humming with chatter as we disrobed.

'The canyons we saw from orbit mean water,' Jack said. 'There was water here, at some point.'

'I'm not disagreeing with the geology,' Elena said, 'and the tidal lock is consistent with the absence of said water now.' The temperature, she meant; any liquid water in Votum's unfailing daylight would've been all too happy to evaporate. 'What I'm wondering is how *that much* water lasted long enough on the surface to create canyons at all.'

Jack *hrm*'d as he hung his helmet. 'Well, what if Votum didn't start out here? What if it orbited further out, had an atmosphere, had a spin, all that good stuff, and something whacked it to where it is now?'

Elena pulled off her socks and nodded. 'A comet, you mean.'

'Sure, or a planet that destroyed itself in the process.'

'That could work.'

Chikondi chimed in. 'But is there any water *left*?' he asked. 'That's what I want to know.'

Elena looked sceptical. 'Not at the surface. It's too hot. And we didn't see any ice caps on the far side.'

Jack scratched his stubble. 'The canyons, though,' he mused. 'They're awfully deep. Could be shady enough for some little puddle to stick around. Or caves, there could be caves. I'm going to put money on caves.'

'You don't have any money,' Elena said.

'Well, if I did, I would. Calling it now: caves.'

Suits vacated, we headed for the ladder. 'If there *are* caves,

I'm not going into one with Ariadne again,' Chikondi said as we climbed.

'What?' I laughed. 'Why?'

'Don't you remember? On Mirabilis?'

I racked my brain, and laughed all the harder at the connection made. There'd been a side pocket in an old lava tube we'd explored that was just about my size, and thus, an impossible-to-resist opportunity to tuck myself inside and wait for Chikondi to walk past. 'Oh, it was funny,' I said. 'You thought it was funny.'

He gave me a facetiously scolding look as we stepped off in the control room. 'It was definitely, definitely not—'

Something in Elena's body language made us shut right up. I followed her gaze to the comms monitor.

The download folder had a number hanging over it.

1, it read.

We circled around.

She pressed play.

The message was not from Earth itself, but the atmospheric border above. I could see my home planet beckoning in the window behind the man on camera, who floated in a room just like the one I stood in. I hadn't realised how deeply I missed the colour green.

'Hey, Lawki 6,' the astronaut said. 'This is Lawki 5.'

'Holy shit, it's Lei,' Jack said. Lei Jian, he meant, one of our colleagues. We knew him – we'd studied together, been to launch parties together. He'd travelled in torpor just as we had, and like us, the years had left their mark on him. I wondered if I'd ever stop feeling shock at a face older than I remembered it.

'I'm going to assume you haven't heard from home either,' Lei said. 'We're pretty sure we know why. We arrived day before yesterday, but there's no signal from the ground. There's no *anything* from the ground. We tried calling the lunar base, and *that* pinged back, but it's an automated signal. Their equipment works, but nobody's home. So we roped in the nearest satellite, and . . . well, it's fried. They all are – nothing's responding to us. We're still gathering info, but everything points toward a massive geomagnetic storm.'

Oh, was my first thought. *Of course*. And then: *Oh. Oh, no. No.*

I don't know how to describe what I felt as the magnitude of what happened dawned on me, without insulting what you on the ground have gone through in the wake of the sun's betrayal. What is my upset, compared with yours? I cannot imagine what you have endured. The technology I live in – the technology Earth built for us – did not fail, has never failed. We have not starved, or frozen. We have not sat shivering in the dark while our food spoiled and our vehicles lay paralysed. And worst of all, we knew this could happen. We've been impotently worrying about what a solar flare could do to electronic infra-structure since the 1900s. But my generation was so preoccupied with fixing the mess left by the unaddressed-and-fully-known-about environmental disaster of the *previous* generation that we committed the same sin of criminal procrastination against yours. I ask no forgiveness for this, because we deserve none. I do not know what conditions were like for you and yours; I can only guess that it has been devastating, given your silence lasting years and not months. How much have you rebuilt? How much could be salvaged?

How many of us are left?

'We're going to land this evening,' Lei said. 'We don't know who'll be down there or if anyone's waiting for us, but the good news is, since *our* comms are working, we'll be able to contact you again once we get the shape of things. Tomorrow, hopefully. Uh, the one thing, though' – his face went wooden as he tried to keep his tone neutral – 'we suffered some damage to our hull somewhere along the way here. Not sure how yet, but we've got a bunch of yellow lights.'

'Oh, God,' I whispered. A damaged hull can mean a lot of things. Some are innocuous. Many are not. One is the possibility of burning up in re-entry. And with no way to call ground crew for support, and no one waiting to pick Lawki 5 up if they needed to eject . . . The astronaut in me had been trained for the risk every one of us faced, had no illusions about our mortality. The human in me couldn't help but feel sick.

Lei's face suggested he mirrored my feelings on both fronts. 'We're sending you all our mission reports, just in case, uh – but really, don't worry. Plan on having drinks with us when you're home, yeah? Be safe out there. We'll call you tomorrow.'

The video ended. I'd never felt the air in that room sit so heavy.

'They could go to the Moon,' Chikondi said. 'They could wait it out there.'

'Wait it out for how long?' Jack said, not unkindly. 'We know how waiting it out goes.'

'I'd want to go home, too,' Elena said. 'I'd want to know. I'd want to help.'

'Besides, there's no telling when the base was abandoned,' I said. 'Functional comms doesn't mean life support is working.' I shook my head, my stomach refusing to settle.

Elena squeezed my shoulder. 'We'll wait for tomorrow,' she said. 'That's all we can do.'

Tomorrow arrived, followed by another, and another, and another.

Lawki 5 did not contact us again.

When the day never ends and the world has no rhythm, it becomes vital for you to make one of your own. I slept like a teenager my first weeks on Votum, letting my body determine its ebb and flow. I did not pay attention to the time on the clock. I drank when thirsty, worked until I needed rest, rested until bored. I never abandoned protocol, but I did not need rigid checklists to follow it. I knew the rules. I knew what needed doing. I wrote myself reminders, not marching orders. I did not chide myself for days in which I did nothing but nap and make a salad, because they were paired with days where I fixed, dug, sampled, studied. Sometimes I went for walks outside – not fieldwork, not exploratory hikes. Just walks. There was a destination I came to enjoy quite by accident – a crumbling ridge overlooking a hypnotisingly flat plain – and no matter where else I wandered to, I often ended up right back there, following the foot-wide trail worn by my steps alone.

I did not feel joy in this simplicity, as I did on Aecor. I don't know what to call the feeling. 'Emptiness' sounds depressing, 'stillness' dull. I think that Votum is like the mirror in my cabin. It doesn't presume anything, doesn't force any decisions. It doesn't angle itself toward me. It just lets me think. I respect it deeply for this.

After each walk, I'd return to the *Merian* coated with a fine layer of red dust, clinging to my suit like a second skin. I loved watching it dance around me in the airlock as the fans brushed it loose. The particles formed murmurations, which gently twisted toward the vents as they were shooed back outside. Every time, as I watched the dirt disappear, as the sterilising plasma wreathed me in swirls of airy purple, I stepped back into my craft feeling a little bit lighter than I had the time before. I know it was only my suit that was cleaned, but something nameless – something that had originated within me – was scattered to the wind along with the dust. Whatever it was, I did not need it back.

Chikondi burst into the cabin, waking both me and Elena. 'Cubesats,' he gasped. He started to say something else, but gave up, frantically gesturing at us. 'Water,' he managed.

We threw on clothes and ran.

Jack was in the data lab, furiously entering commands into the console. 'It's coming in now,' he said.

'What's coming in?' Elena said.

An image spread across the screen: Votum from above, a parched rockface with the occasional accent of airy cloud. I'd seen this patch we were looking at before, a series of canyons the team back home had nicknamed the Furrows. The telescopes in Earth's orbit hadn't been able to see what lay inside them, but *we* could. The grand majority of them were empty – geologic wrinkles, nothing more. But in one, way down deep in the shadows, there lay something promising. A reflective sliver. A filament a casual glance would miss entirely.

We held our breath.

An enormous smile spread across Jack's face. 'Told you,' he whispered.

'This looks like a good landing site,' I said, pointing at a plateau near the canyons. 'I know we just got the lab set up, but—'

Chikondi started gathering everything that wasn't bolted down: styluses, water bottles, someone's jacket. The message was received. We were packing up, and we were doing it *now*.

We launched, and landed.

We set up camp, again.

We left the *Merian* at dawn the next day, and hiked some four kilometres out.

We rappelled down the ancient walls into the shaded dark. The canyon wind whistled past, greeting us ghostily.

We walked for a time, our footsteps echoing in all directions. Had there been such echoes in this canyon before? I wondered. Was the air here accustomed to carrying sounds beyond those it created on its own?

We rounded a corner, and there it was: one thin river – a creek, really, if we're being accurate. It was not in any particular hurry, and would barely have reached my knees if I'd stepped into it. Its surface glinted a mercurial grey in the light of our headlamps. Its meandering pace created a pleasant chatter along the stones it had worn smooth. The irony did not escape me – I'd ached for respite from the aquatic clamour on Opera, yet here, the sound of water was the most welcome thing imaginable.

There was something missing, though, and I could feel our collective mood dip just a touch as we individually registered it. The river had no plants, no moss, no encouraging stripes of scum. Nothing swam beneath its ripples or tiptoed toward the bank in search of a drink. Perhaps the number of living organisms on Votum numbered just four, I thought, and only temporary residents at that.

Chikondi opened his toolkit and knelt down beside the river. He retrieved a field microscope. He dipped it into the water.

We crowded patiently behind him.

The little viewscreen switched on, and the image projected was white, pure white, the same colour as the base of the sample chamber. Chikondi gently rocked the microscope, encouraging other bits of the sample to slide into view. We saw a lump of rock, a shred of silt. That was all right. Finding nothing was all right. There was still so much to learn, even in the absence of—

Out of the bottom left corner, a shape emerged. A jellied blob with tiny structures at its heart, drifting into frame.

We vibrated with noiseless excitement. It was a cell – just one. Simple and superb.

There was a pause, a subtle shudder. The cell split into two.

I can't say that I cheered. I roared. I thundered.

'There it goes!' Jack cried.

'Oh, my God,' Elena said, grinning from ear to ear.

'There it goes!' Jack punched his fists at nothing, the energy within him demanding an exit.

Chikondi simply laughed. He laughed and laughed, filling the gap left by inadequate words.

*

Jack's imaginary money was well placed on caves. We found one tucked into a canyon wall, a low-hanging doorway leading to another realm. We had to crawl on our knees to get through the front passageway, sometimes splashing through the flow, but beyond that, the water had carved a magnificent inner chamber. Lei's River, as we named it, joins two subterranean waterways there, and at their nexus is a glassy pool, chest deep and uncannily serene. Dazzling twists of crystals hang overhead, festooning the ceiling and walls like antique lace. The air in there is warm, thanks to steam vents running beneath the rock, and thoroughly sequestered from the harsh sun's reach. It is the perfect place for life to develop, and, less importantly, for us to work.

As the only macroscopic life forms on Votum (thus far, anyway), we had no compunctions about setting up a field lab within the cave itself. There are no critters to knock it over, no weather to damage it. Everything we brought was sterilised, of course. We tread lightly in this sanctuary. But it is also a place I've come to inhabit fully. For the moment, the cave is home. I think, to answer the question I asked myself on Opera, a home can only exist in a moment. Something both found and made. Always temporary, in the grand scheme of things, but vital all the same.

One day I looked up from my worktable, where I'd been labelling rock samples to take back to the *Merian*. Chikondi was sitting by the pool, like always, watching his tablet intently and humming along with his headphones. He was running some sort of test on the bacterial samples he'd collected; any attempt to ask him what he was up to was answered with a vague mumble that indicated he was in the middle of puzzling something out and would fill us in when the idea was fully formed. Elena and Jack were standing beside a glittering twist of crystal, deep in a congenial argument about something to do with salinity. I admit that I wasn't paying attention to the particulars. I was too busy watching the three of them and myself, each firmly in our elements. The cave is a reflection of us, in its way. Rock, water, and life, all of which need tools to examine them. All of which mean nothing if no one is there to observe.

'We can't go back,' I said.

Elena and Jack looked at me. Chikondi did as well, though it took my comment a half-second longer to register with him.

I knew what I'd said was ridiculous, but the urge to say it had been growing inside me for weeks, and the rest came spilling out after. 'Lawki 5 made it back to Earth, at least. That means everybody else is long since back. And if the Moon's been abandoned, and if there are no functioning satellites, that means nobody is launching anything. We're not the last of the Lawki program out here. We're . . . we're the last. Of anyone.'

Nobody looked as if my words were revelatory. They'd all been thinking this, too. Jack sighed. 'We don't have the equipment to do a long-term study here. Or on Mirabilis, or wherever.'

Chikondi nodded regretfully. 'And the longer we stay,' he said in a measured tone, 'the more disruptive we are. Our visits are limited for a reason. We can't have an influence.' This was OCA ethics, word for word.

'I know,' I said. 'I don't disagree with any of that. I never have.'

Elena looked me in the eye. 'Then what are you saying?'

I took a deep breath. 'The interstellar engine has enough fuel to get back to Earth. Fourteen light-years, with a bit of wiggle room.' I paused, choosing my words, trying to speak slow. 'Thing is, that would also get us to Tivael.'

My words hung in the still air of the cave. Everybody understood what I was saying. Tivael was one of OCA's earliest candidates for the Lawki program, but given its distance from Earth – over thirty light-years, or sixty years in transit – it was ruled out due to the limits of technology and the logistics of time.

From Zhenyi, however, Tivael was only thirteen light-years

away. And I knew, as we all did, that there are three habitable planets in orbit around it. Going by the atmospheric data, life's a near certainty on each of them. In particular, there's one with an awful lot of greenhouse gases in the mix. Could be volcanic activity. Could be the natural state of things.

Could be something else.

Jack paced. 'We . . .' He stopped and thought. Like me, he was treading carefully. 'Okay.' He stuck his thumbs behind his toolbelt. 'You're saying that if we're the last astronauts – the last *at all* – then we should prolong our mission, so that this kind of work will continue in the interim while Earth gets back on its feet.'

'Yes.'

He gave a single nod. 'What's your evidence that OCA is gone, and that they're not planning to rebuild?' The question was delivered objectively, professorially. He was challenging my suggestion, as he rightly should.

'I have none.'

'What's your evidence that there are no other humans in space besides us, right now?'

'I have none.'

'And why Tivael?'

'Because we can,' I said. I gestured around. 'Why *here*?'

Chikondi nodded at that, but his attention was split, one eye still on his tablet as data compiled.

Jack continued. 'So, you're saying that even though we have no idea what's going on back home, and can only speculate as to the current state of Earth's spaceflight capabilities, in order to further the . . . the spirit of the mission we were sent here for, we should break the mission parameters entirely.'

'Yes.'

Elena joined in. She leaned against the wall, arms crossed. 'Even though we'd never go back. We'd never see Earth again.'

'Yes.'

She looked at me hard. 'We might live longer than our time on those worlds would allow for.'

'I know.'

'And if we did simply live out our lives, we'd do it in the *Merian,* off-planet.'

'I know.'

'Life support wasn't intended to last through a second mission. We could die *before* our work there is done.'

I returned the look. 'So, you're saying we'll either die old and housebound, or relatively young, in some kind of accident or disaster.' I let that sit. 'Those are the same options we'd get on Earth.'

She gave the smallest of smirks.

Jack paced more ardently. 'Okay, but *we* didn't make the decision to come out here. Thousands of people all over the world made that call. Do we have the . . . the . . . fuck, I don't know – the *right* to decide this?'

'Those thousands of people wanted this work done,' Elena said.

'Yeah, but those thousands of people are mostly dead,' Jack replied. 'We can't say we're doing this work *for Earth* if the Earth that's out there now didn't give us their thumbs up. We'd be doing it for ourselves.'

'*Would* we be doing this for ourselves?' Elena asked. 'I'm fine dying out here, in concept, but I *am* looking forward to going back. I didn't sign up for a one-way trip. None of us did. I'm not saying yes to this at all, I'm exploring the—'

'Yes!' cried Chikondi. 'Oh, my – oh, my God. Oh, my God.' He gestured frantically at his tablet, his body about to explode. 'Everybody, please, come look, come look.'

'What is it?' I said, as we drifted over.

Chikondi held his screen up to us, his test results complete. 'Look, look, *look*,' he said.

My eyes scanned over the dense table of numbers and letters. I didn't see it at first.

Elena saw it. She covered her mouth with her hand in surprise, but her smile was so big it inched out past her fingers.

Jack saw it. 'Holy *shit*,' he said.

The connection clicked. I saw it, too. 'Oh,' I gasped. 'Oh, they're—'

Chikondi beamed at us, his face reverent. 'Look what we found.'

For a brief time in my life, I was ambidextrous. I remember a craft project in preschool where we were tasked with cutting shapes out of thick, coloured paper. My right hand quickly tired, my fingers cramped and weary within the confines of the handle (I imagine, in hindsight, that I'd been at it for all of five minutes). But this was no problem. I merely swapped the scissors into my left hand, and continued along. I wish I could still perform this trick, but alas, a teacher made me pick a side when we began to learn to write the alphabet. I chose right, because most kids used their right, and this seemed the least bother. The left has never served me well again. I don't blame it for holding a grudge.

Molecules have a 'handedness' as well. This is called chirality, and if you've never encountered this concept before, it's one of those that can make you sit back and stare into the distance for a while. I'll walk you through it as simply as I can.

Take a moment to look at your hands (assuming that you have two; if you do not, borrow someone else's, for science). Stretch them out and splay your fingers. Both hands, naturally, are made up of the same parts: wrist, palm, fingers, knuckles, nails. Matching ingredient lists. The exact same equipment.

If I were to give you a right-handed glove, you would not be able to wear it on your left hand. It wouldn't matter how you flipped or twisted your appendage around. You might be able to cram your fingers in there, but the fit would be terrible, and you wouldn't be able to use the glove properly. Even though your left hand has the same physical parts as your right, it will never, ever be the same shape.

The same is true for molecules. If you take two identical mixes of atoms and arrange them so that they are mirror-image configurations of each other, the molecules you've created are no longer the same thing, and the differences in how they interact with the world can be as different as night and day. To use the most famous (and disastrous) example of this, consider thalidomide, a compound that was widely prescribed to treat morning sickness in the 1950s. While right-handed thalidomide does indeed ease those symptoms, its left-handed twin causes severe birth defects. Chirality is a detail not to be ignored.

As a rule, life on Earth uses left-handed amino acids and right-handed sugars. This is an age-old puzzle of biochemistry, one that bleeds out into many adjacent fields. One can safely assume that when life began, it utilised whatever organic compounds were directly in front of it. Now, *right-handed* amino acids and *left-handed* sugars can easily be created in a lab. Anytime you whip up a batch of these things, you can expect an even spread of handedness. So, why, then, does life on Earth have a bias? Why would it feed on one and not the other, if both should have been naturally available? Why would there be *only* left-handed amino acids and right-handed sugars in the spot where our single-celled ancestors woke up?

The most likely answer is meteorites. We know that space rocks carry organic compounds aplenty, and if one of these smacks into a planet, it serves as something akin to a seed bomb lobbed into a vacant lot. If such a rock landed on Earth, and if, by either chance or the intricacies of chemistry, it carried mostly left-handed amino acids, you can see how life that developed in that delivery site might get accustomed to such homogeneity and pass that template on to its offspring.

But what if, instead, a handed preference is merely an intrinsic quality of life? What if life just *works* that way, for reasons we've yet to untangle? For a long time, we had only a single test subject to work with – the Earth – and any scientist will tell you it's impossible to determine anything from a sample size of one.

As we branched out to other worlds, the species we found also exhibited rigid preferences one way or the other. Life on Aecor is Earth's opposite: right-handed amino acids and left-handed sugars are the norm there. Life on Mirabilis prefers everything left-handed. The findings from Lawki 5 are in concert with this; everything they found leaned one way or the other. This confirmed the suspicion that life does not have to arise under the exact same conditions as life on Earth, but it doesn't answer the underlying question: are meteorites responsible for chiral preferences in life, or is a chiral preference a *requirement* of life?

In the pool in the cave carved by Lei's River, Chikondi sampled one hundred species of single-celled organisms. None of them possess a chiral preference. They freely use amino acids and sugars of both types. They are, in effect, ambidextrous. And when Elena tested the water and Jack tested the rock, their findings confirmed what Chikondi's indicated: the chirality of amino acids on Votum exists in a balanced ratio.

This means that chiral preference is *not* a requirement of life.

This means that emergent life forms *do* use whatever is on hand.

This strongly suggests that life on Earth only arose thanks to ingredients that originated off-planet.

This further suggests that life in the galaxy typically *does* rely on concentrated deliveries of organic molecules via meteorite in order to get started, but this is not the only way it can happen.

Now, to be fair, we're basing that hypothesis on the Lawki data, which represents only a handful of planets. We would need a larger sample size to be sure.

If you are a person of science – whether it be your career or your hobby or a passing interest – I would imagine this fact ignites you as it did us. We haven't answered the biggest Why yet, but damned if we didn't get a step closer.

But what if science isn't your world? I admit, I don't know whether people outside of my social sphere would care about this at all. I've spent my entire adult life embedded with scientists and the people who love them. I take it for granted that this sort of knowledge is cherished, is yearned for. And I am keenly aware that in order to tell you what we found, it required a thousand words of explanation before I could get to the crux. Is this discovery of ours too obtuse? Did you skim through the science in search of the point? I won't judge you if you did; I'm genuinely curious. Facts about amino acid chirality will affect nothing in your daily life. They won't put food on the table. They won't build a roof over your head. They won't strengthen your relationships or keep you healthy or help you do your chores. They change nothing about the everyday. But what I hope is that when you're lying in the dark and wondering – when you're asking that big Why – what we found will help you fall asleep with the comfort of a little more context than you had before.

Does it? Or am I wrong? Are we out here chasing useless things? I can't escape my bias, just as my cells can't use right-handed amino acids. I want to know whether you care about our arcane work in the sky, given your immediate struggles on the ground. I will not be upset by the answer. I just want to know. All of us aboard the *Merian* want to know what *you* want of us.

So, here's how this is going to go.

After I finish writing this, and after my crewmates give it their approval, and after we send the file back to Earth, we're going to finish our remaining three-and-a-half years on Votum. After that, we're going into torpor.

Where we go from there is up to you.

I've reconfigured the *Merian*'s torpor system so that it will keep us asleep until the craft receives a message from Earth. We've provided the technical transmission instructions separately, but essentially, the *Merian* will be awaiting a simple yes or no.

'Yes' sends us to Tivael.

'No' takes us back to Earth.

If we receive no answer, we'll remain in torpor until old age or equipment failure takes us.

We are comfortable with any of these scenarios.

What we want you to ask yourselves is this: what is space, to you? Is it a playground? A quarry? A flagpole? A classroom? A temple? Who do you believe should go, and for what purpose? Or should we go at all? Is the realm above the clouds immaterial to you, so long as satellites send messages and rocks don't fall? Is human spaceflight a fool's errand, a rich man's fantasy, an unacceptable waste of life and metal? Are our methods grotesque to you, our ethics untenable? Are our hopes outdated? When I tell you of our life out here, do you cheer for us, or do you scoff?

Are astronauts still relevant in your time?

We have found nothing you can sell. We have found nothing you can put to practical use. We have found no worlds that could be easily or ethically settled, were that end desired. We have satisfied nothing but curiosity, gained nothing but knowledge.

To me, these are the noblest goals. The people who sent us here believed the same. But if you share that belief, do you understand that we might fail? You must understand the cost here – the reality of what we do. Because sometimes we go, and we try, and we suffer, and despite it all, we learn nothing. Sometimes we are left with more questions than when we started. Sometimes we do harm, despite our best efforts. We are human. We are fragile. Are we who you want out here? Would you be more comfortable with the limited predictability of machines? Or is the flexibility of human intelligence worth the risk of our minds and bodies breaking?

We believe the potential answers are worth the challenges. We do not know what you believe, what Earth believes. And ultimately, it is Earth that sent us. Four people alone cannot decide whether it is right for us to venture further into the galaxy, desperately as we want to. I don't operate under the delusion that OCA represented – *represents*, if you're still there – all of humanity. But space travel is a grand enough venture, a daunting enough task, that it requires the dedication of the many, not the mere fervour of a few. We are four. It took the work of thousands to get us here, and the resources of thousands more. Our days out here have been largely autonomous, but we live within a home that was lovingly built by other hands. Everything we do, we do on the shoulders of others. And for that reason, a consensus of four is insufficient. If no one is listening, if no one cares, then we would be staying out here only for ego. We will have abandoned you, and that's unacceptable to us.

We are ready to live out our lives without ever seeing Earth again. We're happy to do it. It is the most natural end I can imagine, the best death I could hope for. But we can't accept that fate if no one is ready to pick up where we left off. If we die out here with your blessing, then we die as your family. If we die without it, we die alone. And if that is the case, we *would* rather come home. We feel it is better, in that scenario, to spend our remaining years in your company, sharing our stories in the hopes that we might relight the spark. Either way, we will carry this torch. All we're asking is: where will it burn brightest?

We leave that question to you.

As the Secretary General of the United Nations, an organisation of one hundred and forty seven member states who represent almost all of the human inhabitants of the planet Earth, I send greetings on behalf of the people of our planet. We step out of our solar system into the universe seeking only peace and friendship – to teach, if we are called upon; to be taught, if we are fortunate. We know full well that our planet and all its inhabitants are but a small part of this immense universe that surrounds us, and it is with humility and hope that we take this step.

– Former UN Secretary General Kurt Waldheim, 1977, as recorded on the Voyager Golden Record

ACKNOWLEDGEMENTS

Like Ariadne, I'm not a scientist. I have no experience in that field of work, nor any formal education within it. Science fiction is my transformative fandom, and as in all heartfelt fic, I revere the canon but play fast and loose with details of my choosing. Still, for this book, I wanted to be as close to the mark as the story would allow, and to that end, I received some help that deserves proper thanks.

In early 2018, I was a guest at the Melon conference in Hong Kong, and it was there – at a welcome reception, blindingly jet-lagged – that I met Lisa Nip, a PhD candidate at MIT Media Lab with a bold goal: using synthetic biology to solve the challenges of human space travel. She gave a talk on that topic the next day, and I sat in the audience, still jet-lagged but on the bleeding edge of my seat. Her vision of genetic engineering as practical supplementation, rather than dystopian eugenics or transhumanist evolution, is one I found both radical and beautiful, and without her blowing my mind wide open, this book wouldn't exist at all. Lisa took the time to Skype with me from her lab while I was in the early stages of figuring everything out, and I am enormously grateful for her generosity and patience in walking me through her science and the possibilities therein. If anything in this story strays too far from the realm of reality, that's a reflection of me coming at this from the sidelines, not of her fine teaching.

This book is likewise better for the counsel of astrobiology educator Nicoline Chambers, my long-time science advisor (and, y'know, my mom), who never seems to tire of my sloppy late-night emails about whether I should use this term or that, whether my planets make sense, and so on. Among my many questions was that of what gear the Lawki 6 crew would bring along for the ride. The *Merian's* labs were stocked by both her and her colleagues Charles Cockell, professor of astrobiology at the University of Edinburgh, and Caroline Williams, assistant professor of integrative biology at UC Berkeley. My thanks to them for helping me assemble a shopping list.

I also must give a hat tip to some folks who I don't know at all but would be very happy to have a beer with. My inspiration for OCA came in part from real-world citizen-funded spaceflight efforts, whose creativity and tenacity sets me on fire. If this concept appeals to you, I encourage you to check out the ongoing work of Copenhagen Suborbitals, Pacific Spaceflight, and the Planetary Society's LightSail project.

As always, this book wouldn't be a book at all if it weren't for the people who unfairly do not have their names on the cover despite all their hard work: Sam Bradbury, Oliver Johnson, David Pomerico, and the amazing teams at both Hodder & Stoughton and Harper Voyager.

Most importantly, love to my family, love to my friends, and love to my wife, all of whom kept me upright through a beast of a year. I'd be lost without you.

Not ready to land back on Earth?

• •

Turn the page for a short extract from
Becky Chamber's debut novel

THE LONG WAY TO A SMALL, ANGRY PLANET

TRANSIT

As she woke up in the pod, she remembered three things. First, she was traveling through open space. Second, she was about to start a new job, one she could not screw up. Third, she had bribed a government official into giving her a new identity file. None of this information was new, but it wasn't pleasant to wake up to.

She wasn't supposed to be awake yet, not for another day at least, but that was what you got for booking cheap transport. Cheap transport meant a cheap pod flying on cheap fuel, and cheap drugs to knock you out. She had flickered into consciousness several times since launch – surfacing in confusion, falling back just as she'd gotten a grasp on things. The pod was dark, and there were no navigational screens. There was no way to tell how much time had passed between each waking, or how far she'd traveled, or if she'd even been traveling at all. The thought made her anxious, and sick.

Her vision cleared enough for her to focus on the window. The shutters were down, blocking out any possible light sources. She knew there were none. She was out in the open now. No bustling planets, no travel lanes, no sparkling orbiters. Just emptiness, horrible emptiness, filled with nothing but herself and the occasional rock.

The engine whined as it prepared for another sublayer jump. The drugs reached out, tugging her down into uneasy sleep. As she faded, she thought again of the job, the lies, the smug look on the official's face as she'd poured credits into his account. She wondered if it had been enough. It had to be. It had to. She'd paid too much already for mistakes she'd had no part in.

Her eyes closed. The drugs took her. The pod, presumably, continued on.

A COMPLAINT

Living in space was anything but quiet. Grounders never expected that. For anyone who had grown up planetside, it took some time to get used to the clicks and hums of a ship, the ever-present ambiance that came with living inside a piece of machinery. But to Ashby, those sounds were as ordinary as his own heartbeat. He could tell when it was time to wake by the sigh of the air filter over his bed. When rocks hit the outer hull with their familiar pattering, he knew which were small enough to ignore, and which meant trouble. He could tell by the amount of static crackling over the ansible how far away he was from the person on the other end. These were the sounds of spacer life, an under-score of vulnerability and distance. They were reminders of what a fragile thing it was to be alive. But those sounds also meant safety. An absence of sound meant that air was no longer flowing, engines no longer running, artigrav nets no longer holding your feet to the floor. Silence belonged to the vacuum outside. Silence was death.

There were other sounds, too, sounds made not by the ship itself, but by the people living in it. Even in the endless halls of homestead ships, you could hear the echoes of nearby conversa-tions, footsteps on metal floors, the faint thumping of a tech climbing through the walls, off to repair some unseen circuit. Ashby's ship, the *Wayfarer*, was spacious enough, but tiny compared to the homesteader he'd grown up on. When he'd first purchased the *Wayfarer* and filled it with crew, even he'd had to get used to the close quarters they kept. But the constant sounds

3

of people working and laughing and fighting all around him had become a comfort. The open was an empty place to be, and there were moments when even the most seasoned spacer might look to the star-flecked void outside with humility and awe.

Ashby welcomed the noise. It was reassuring to know that he was never alone out there, especially given his line of work. Building wormholes was not a glamorous profession. The interspatial passageways that ran throughout the Galactic Commons were so ordinary as to be taken for granted. Ashby doubted the average person gave tunneling much more thought than you might give a pair of pants or a hot cooked meal. But his job required him to think about tunnels, and to think hard on them, at that. If you sat and thought about them for too long, imagined your ship diving in and out of space like a needle pulling thread . . . well, that was the sort of thinking that made a person glad for some noisy company.

Ashby was in his office, reading a news feed over a cup of mek, when one particular sound made him cringe. Footsteps. Corbin's footsteps. Corbin's *angry* footsteps, coming right toward his door. Ashby sighed, swallowed his irritation, and became the captain. He kept his face neutral, his ears open. Talking to Corbin always required a moment of preparation, and a good deal of detachment.

Artis Corbin was two things: a talented algaeist and a complete asshole. The former trait was crucial on a long-haul ship like the *Wayfarer*. A batch of fuel going brown could be the difference between arriving at port and going adrift. Half of one of the *Wayfarer's* lower decks was filled with nothing but algae vats, all of which needed someone to obsessively adjust their nutrient content and salinity. This was one area in which Corbin's lack of social graces was actually a benefit. The man *preferred* to stay cooped up in the algae bay all day, muttering over readouts, working in pursuit of what he called 'optimal conditions.' Conditions always seemed optimal enough to Ashby, but he wasn't going to get in Corbin's way where algae was concerned. Ashby's fuel costs had dropped by ten percent since he brought Corbin aboard, and there were few algaeists who would accept a position on a tunneling ship in the first place. Algae could be touchy enough on a short trip, but keeping your batches healthy over a long haul required meticulousness, and stamina, too. Corbin hated people, but he loved his work, and he was damn good at it. In Ashby's book, that made him extremely valuable. An extremely valuable headache.

The door spun open and Corbin stormed in. His brow was beaded with sweat, as usual, and the graying hair at his temples looked slick. The *Wayfarer* had to be kept warm for their pilot's sake, but Corbin had voiced his dislike for the ship's standard temperature from day one. Even after years aboard the ship, his body had refused to acclimate, seemingly out of pure spite.

Corbin's cheeks were red as well, though whether that was due to his mood or from coming up the stairs was anyone's guess. Ashby never got used to the sight of cheeks that red. The majority of living Humans were descended from the Exodus Fleet, which had sailed far beyond the reaches of their ancestral sun. Many, like Ashby, had been born within the very same homesteaders that had belonged to the original Earthen refugees. His tight black curls and amber skin were the result of generations of mingling and mixing aboard the giant ships. Most Humans, whether space-born or colony kids, shared that nationless Exodan blend.

Corbin, on the other hand, was unmistakably Sol system stock, even though the people of the home planets had come to resemble Exodans in recent generations. With as much of a hodgepodge as Human genetics were, lighter shades were known to pop up here and there, even in the Fleet. But Corbin was practically *pink*. His forerunners had been scientists, early explorers who built the first research orbiters around Enceladus. They'd been there for centuries, keeping vigil over the bacteria flourishing within icy seas. With Sol a dim thumbprint in the skies above Saturn, the researchers lost more and more pigment with every decade. The end result was Corbin, a pink man bred for tedious labwork and a sunless sky.

Corbin tossed his scrib over Ashby's desk. The thin, rectangular pad sailed through the mist-like pixel screen and clattered down in front of Ashby. Ashby gestured to the pixels, instructing them to disperse. The news headlines hovering in the air dissolved into colored wisps. The pixels slunk down like swarms of tiny insects into the projector boxes on either side of the desk. Ashby looked at the scrib, and raised his eyebrows at Corbin.

'*This*,' Corbin said, pointing a bony finger at the scrib, 'has got to be a joke.'

'Let me guess,' Ashby said. 'Jenks messed with your notes again?' Corbin frowned and shook his head. Ashby focused on the scrib, trying not to laugh at the memory of the last time Jenks had hacked into Corbin's scrib, replacing the algaeist's careful notes with three-hundred-and-sixty-two photographic variations of Jenks himself, naked as the day he was born. Ashby had thought the one of Jenks carrying a Galactic Commons banner was particularly good. It had a sort of dramatic dignity to it, all things considered.

Ashby picked up the scrib, flipping it screen-side up.

Attn.: Captain Ashby Santoso (Wayfarer, GC tunneling license no. 387-97456)
Re: Resume for Rosemary Harper (GC administration certificate no. 65-78-2)

Ashby recognized the file. It was the resume for their new clerk, who was scheduled to arrive the next day. She was probably strapped into a deepod by now, sedated for the duration of her long, cramped trip. 'Why are you showing me this?' Ashby asked.

'Oh, so you *have* actually read it,' Corbin said.

'Of course I have. I told you all to read this file ages ago so you could get a feel for her before she arrived.' Ashby had no idea what Corbin was getting at, but this was Corbin's standard operating procedure. Complain first, explain later.

Corbin's reply was predictable, even before he opened his mouth: 'I didn't have the time.' Corbin had a habit of ignoring tasks that didn't originate within his lab. 'What the hell are you thinking, bringing aboard a kid like that?'

'I was thinking,' Ashby said, 'that I need a certified clerk.' Even Corbin couldn't argue that point. Ashby's records were a mess, and while a tunneling ship didn't strictly *need* a clerk in order to keep its license, the suits at the GC Transportation Board had made it pretty clear that Ashby's perpetually late reports weren't earning him any favors. Feeding and paying an extra crew member was no small expense, but after careful consideration and some nudging from Sissix, Ashby had asked the board to send him someone certified. His business was going to start suffering if he didn't stop trying to do two jobs at once.

Corbin folded his arms and sniffed. 'Have you talked to her?'

'We had a sib chat last tenday. She seems fine.'

'*She seems fine,*' Corbin repeated. 'That's encouraging.'

Ashby chose his next words more carefully. This was Corbin, after all. The king of semantics. 'The Board cleared her. She's fully qualified.'

'The Board is smoking smash.' He stabbed his finger toward the scrib again. 'She's got no long haul experience. She's never lived off Mars, as far as I can tell. She's fresh out of university—'

Ashby started ticking things off on his fingers. Two could play at this game. 'She's certified to handle GC formwork. She's worked an internship at a ground transport company, which required the same basic skills I need her to have. She's fluent in Hanto, gestures and all, which could really open some doors for us. She comes with a letter of recommendation from her interspecies relations professor. And most importantly, from the little I've spoken to her, she seems like someone I can work with.'

'She's never done this before. We're out in the middle of the open, on our way to a blind punch, and you're bringing a *kid* aboard.'

'She's not a kid, she's just young. And everybody has a first job, Corbin. Even you must've started somewhere.'

'You know what my first job was? Scrubbing out sample dishes in my father's lab. A trained *animal* could have done that job. *That's* what a first job should be, not—' He sputtered. 'May I remind you of what we do here? We fly around punching holes – very literal holes – through space. This is not a safe job. Kizzy and Jenks scare the hell out of me with their carelessness as it is, but at least they're experienced. I can't do my job if I'm constantly worried about some incompetent rookie pushing the wrong button.'

That was the warning flag, the *I can't work under these conditions* flag that indicated Corbin was about to go nonlinear. It was time to get him back on the rails. 'Corbin, she's not going to be pushing any buttons. She's not doing anything more complicated than writing reports and filing formwork.'

'*And* liasing with border guards, and planetary patrols, and clients who are late on their payments. The people we have to work with are not all nice people. They are not all *trustworthy* people. We need someone who can hold their own, who can bark down some upstart deputy who thinks he knows regulations better than us. Somebody who knows the difference between a *real* food safety stamp and a smuggler's knock-off. Somebody who actually knows how things *work* out here, not some blank-eyed graduate who will wet herself the first time a Quelin enforcer pulls up alongside.'

Ashby set his mug down. 'What *I* need,' he said, 'is someone to keep my records accurate. I need someone to manage our appointments, to make sure we all get the required vaccinations and scans before crossing borders, and to get my financial files sorted out. It's a complicated job, but not a difficult one, not if she's as organized as her letter of recommendation makes her out to be.'

'That's a standardized letter if ever I saw one. I bet that professor has sent the exact same letter on behalf of every milquetoast student that came mewling through his door.'

Ashby arched an eyebrow. 'She studied at Alexandria University, same as you.'

Corbin scoffed. 'I was in the science department. There's a difference.'

Ashby gave a short laugh. 'Sissix is right, Corbin, you *are* a snob.'

'Sissix can go to hell.'

'So I heard you telling her last night. I could hear you down the hall.' Corbin and Sissix were going to kill each other one of these days. They had never gotten along, and neither of them had any interest in trying to find a common ground. It was an area where Ashby had to tread very lightly. Ashby and Sissix had been friends before the *Wayfarer*, but when he was in captain mode, both she and Corbin had to be treated equally as members of his crew. Moderating their frequent sparring matches required a delicate approach. Most of the time, he tried to stay out of it altogether. 'Should I even ask?'

Corbin's mouth twitched. 'She used the last of my dentbots.'

Ashby blinked. 'You do know we've got huge cases of dentbot packs down in the cargo bay.'

'Not *my* dentbots. You buy those cheap hackjob bots that leave your gums sore.'

'I use those bots every day and my gums feel just fine.'

'I have sensitive gums. You can ask Dr Chef for my dental records if you don't believe me. I have to buy my own bots.'

Ashby hoped that his face did not reveal just how low this tale of woe ranked on his list of priorities. 'I appreciate that it's annoying, but it's just one pack of dentbots we're talking about here.'

Corbin was indignant. 'They don't come cheap! She did it just to get at me, I know she did. If that selfish lizard can't—'

'Hey!' Ashby sat up straight. 'Not okay. I don't want to hear that word come out of your mouth again.' As far as racial insults went, *lizard* was hardly the worst, but it was bad enough.

Corbin pressed his lips together, as if to keep further unpleasantries from escaping. 'Sorry.'

Ashby's hackles were up, but truthfully, this was an ideal way for a conversation with Corbin to go. Get him away from the crew, let him vent, wait for him to cross a line, then talk him down while he was feeling penitent. 'I will talk to Sissix, but you have got to be more civil to people. And I don't care how mad you get, that kind of language does not belong on my ship.'

'I just lost my temper, was all.' Corbin was obviously still angry, but even he knew better than to bite the hand that feeds. Corbin knew that he was a valuable asset, but at the end of the day, Ashby was the one who sent credits to his account. *Valuable* was not the same as *irreplaceable*.

'Losing your temper is one thing, but you are part of a multispecies crew, and you need to be mindful of that. Especially with somebody new coming aboard. And on that note, I'm sorry you have concerns about her, but frankly, she's not your problem. Rosemary was the Board's suggestion, but agreeing to take her on was my call. If she's a mistake, we'll get someone new. But until then, we are all going to give her the benefit of the doubt. Regardless of how you feel about her, I expect you to make her feel welcome. In fact . . .' A slow smile spread across Ashby's face.

Corbin looked wary. 'What?'

Ashby leaned back in his chair, lacing his fingers together. 'Corbin, I seem to recall that our new clerk will be arriving around seventeen-half tomorrow. Now, I have a sib scheduled with Yoshi at seventeen on the nose, and you know how he loves to talk. I doubt I'll be done by the time Rosemary docks, and she's going to need someone to show her around.'

'Oh, no.' A stricken look crossed Corbin's face. 'Have Kizzy do it. She loves that sort of thing.'

'Kizzy's got her hands full replacing the air filter by the med bay, and I doubt she'll be done before tomorrow. Jenks will be helping Kizzy, so he's out.'

'Sissix, then.'

'Mmm, Sissix has a lot of prep work to do before the punch tomorrow. She probably won't have the time.' Ashby grinned. 'I'm sure you'll give her a great tour.'

Corbin looked at his employer with baleful eyes. 'Sometimes you're a real pain in the ass, Ashby.'

Ashby picked up his mug and finished off the dregs. 'I knew I could count on you.'

Not ready to come back to Earth?

Immerse yourself in Becky Chambers'
Sunday Times **bestselling series of standalone novels.**

'The best speculative fiction currently
being written'

John Connolly, *Sunday Times* bestselling author

'A quietly profound, humane tour de force'

Guardian

'Chambers is simply an exceptional talent'

Tor.com

OUT NOW

WANT MORE?

If you enjoyed this and would like to find out about similar books we publish, we'd love you to join our online Sci-Fi, Fantasy and Horror community, Hodderscape.

Visit hodderscape.co.uk for exclusive content form our authors, news, competitions and general musings, and feel free to comment, contribute or just keep an eye on what we are up to.

See you there!

HODDERSCAPE
NEVER AFRAID TO BE OUT OF THIS WORLD

 @Hodderscape  @Hodderscape /hodderscape